The GARDEN of LOST SECRETS

D0191133

To my family

First published in the UK in 2019 by Usborne Publishing Ltd., Usborne House, 83-85 Saffron Hill, London EC1N 8RT, England. www.usborne.com

Copyright © Ann-Marie Howell, 2019.

The right of Ann-Marie Howell to be identified as the author of this work has been asserted by her in accordance with the Copyright, Designs and Patents Act, 1988.

Cover, inside illustrations and map by Amy Grimes © Usborne Publishing, 2019.

Photo of Ann-Marie Howell © Nick Ilott Photography, 2019.

The name Usborne and the devices ♀ ⊕ are Trade Marks of Usborne Publishing Ltd.

A CIP catalogue record for this book is available from the British Library.

JFMAMJJAS ND/19   05231/6   ISBN: 9781474959551

Printed in the UK

The GARDEN of LOST SECRETS

A. M. HOWELL

USBORNE

Contents

Chapter 1	New Home	9
Chapter 2	The Boy	15
Chapter 3	Locked Door	21
Chapter 4	Hothouse	29
Chapter 5	Milky-eyed Man	38
Chapter 6	Search for the Boy	45
Chapter 7	Homesick	50
Chapter 8	The Mandarin	57
Chapter 9	Will	64
Chapter 10	Stolen Fruit	71
Chapter 11	Tiger the Dog	77
Chapter 12	Keyhole	86
Chapter 13	Notebook	91
Chapter 14	Brothers	100
Chapter 15	The Tapestry	108
Chapter 16	The Key	115
Chapter 17	Will's Plan	122
Chapter 18	Pineapples	129
Chapter 19	War Office	135
Chapter 20	The Soldier	141

Chapter 21	Letters	151
Chapter 22	Delivery	160
Chapter 23	Hospital Blues	169
Chapter 24	Abbeygate Street	176
Chapter 25	Parcel for Will	182
Chapter 26	Being Brave	190
Chapter 27	The Basket	196
Chapter 28	A Dreadful Business	203
Chapter 29	The Thief	210
Chapter 30	Locked Up	217
Chapter 31	The Hall Boy	228
Chapter 32	In the Cellars	234
Chapter 33	The Big House	242
Chapter 34	The Earl	248
Chapter 35	A Stormy Night	253
Chapter 36	Clara's Envelope	260
Chapter 37	Courage	268
Chapter 38	Zeppelin	275
Chapter 39	Luck	281
Chapter 40	Scarlet Brazilian	287

Author's Note

Book Club Questions

Usborne Quicklinks

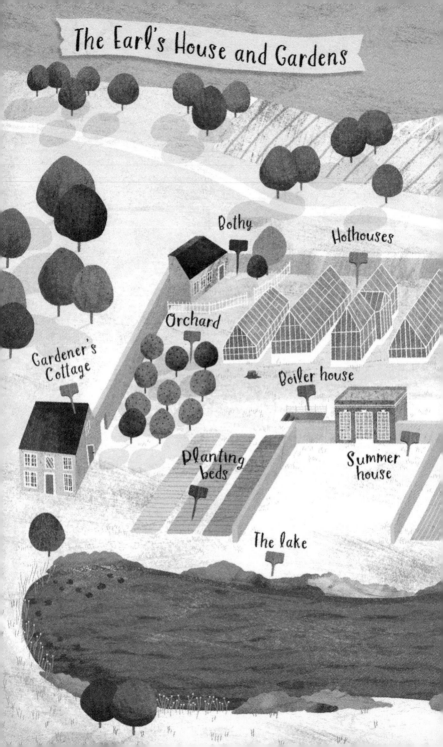

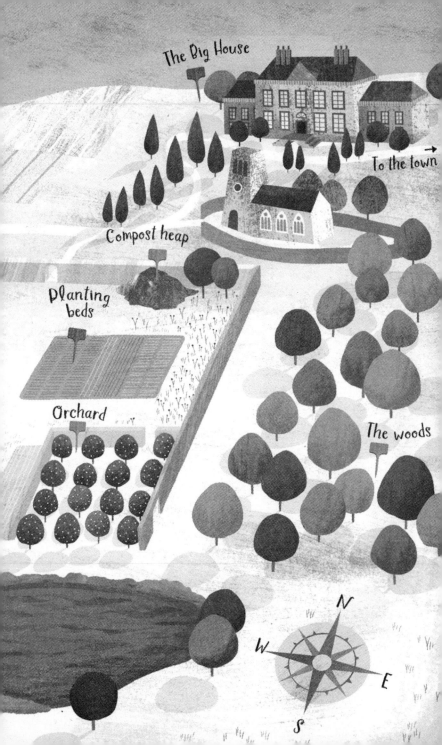

The Big House

To the town

Compost heap

Planting beds

Orchard

The woods

N
W   E
S

CHAPTER I

New Home

Clara's secret weighed heavy in the pocket of her pinafore apron, as her boots crunched down the gravel path to Gardener's Cottage. Her nose crinkled. It was a house that didn't look like a house. One end of the cottage was built into a high red-brick wall which enclosed three sides of the kitchen gardens, separating them from the rest of the Earl's grand country estate. A brown door was fitted into the wall at an angle, like a picture which had been given a gentle push to the right and never been straightened. Above it, a diamond-paned window gazed like a watchful eye over the sloping patchwork of vegetable plots, tumbledown scarecrows and apple trees weighed with fruit.

Mrs Gilbert, the Earl's housekeeper, trudged up the path ahead of Clara. Her wavy speckled-with-grey hair was pinned neatly under her cloth hat. Clara patted at her own hair. Her auburn curls fell messily over her shoulders. Was that why Mrs Gilbert's forehead had puckered when she had arrived?

Clara turned and stared into the gardens. They were larger than the largest park in her home town, sloped this way and that as if the ground could not make up its mind which way to go. Along the southern perimeter of the gardens there was no walled boundary, but there was a small lake which shimmered in the early October sun. Four glass hothouses of varying sizes stood in the centre. Condensation steamed up the large windows, fat leaves pressing against them like they were trying to escape. A man with a stooped back was whistling loudly and out of tune as he pushed a barrow-load of burnt-orange pumpkins and green marrows along a path between the hothouses towards her. Two younger men were chatting in the orchard, the rise and fall of their voices chiming with the soft thud of apples as they dropped them into wicker baskets. To her left, another man was huffing and puffing as his fork turned over the soil in a planting bed.

Just then, the man pushing the barrow saw Clara looking and gave her a cheery wave.

She was about to wave in reply when Mrs Gilbert's voice, tight with irritation, rang across the gardens. "Come along, Clara."

The man with the barrow lowered his head and walked on.

Mrs Gilbert opened the brown door. It was unlocked. Clara's throat tightened, as did her grasp on her secret, as she followed Mrs Gilbert into a dingy hallway.

Clara swallowed and put her small case down on the tiled floor. At the end of the hall stood a man whose coal-black bushy hair tickled the low cottage ceiling. He pushed a notebook and stubby pencil into his trouser pocket and gave Mrs Gilbert a soft look filled with words which Clara didn't understand. He sighed. Sorrow? Disappointment? Something else entirely? Whichever it was, Clara was certain it was somehow connected with her arrival.

"You remember Mr Gilbert, my husband?" Mrs Gilbert said in a thin voice.

Clara nodded and did her best to force her lips into a smile. It had been 1913 when the Gilberts had last been to visit Clara and her family in Kent. That was

11

three years ago, and she had only a handful of memories of this man whose ruddy middle-aged cheeks told a story of a life spent outdoors working as the head gardener on the Earl's estate. A piggyback ride around the park on a blustery day. The telling-off from her mother when she and Mr Gilbert had dipped their fingers into a pan of still-warm blackcurrant jam. The deep grooves in his cheeks from his near-permanent smile. Clara swallowed. The grooves were still there but the smile wasn't. "Hello," she said. Her voice was dry and cracked after her two long train journeys.

Mr Gilbert nodded. He stood and looked at Clara for a few seconds. "Welcome," he said. His voice reminded Clara of her mother's coconut cake – slightly gritty but edged with softness. He opened his mouth as if to say something else, then, apparently thinking better of it, he turned, his hair gathering a drifting cobweb on the ceiling (and perhaps a dead fly or two) and disappeared through another door at the end of the hall. The sound of cupboard doors opening and shutting, a table being laid for tea, made Mrs Gilbert purse her lips and fiddle with the cuffs of her navy woollen jacket.

Clara glanced at the remains of the cobweb swaying in the breeze from the still-open front door behind her.

It wasn't the welcome her parents had said she would get or that she had been expecting. Her shoulders sagged.

"Keep away from the woods. The Earl is allowing the Suffolk Rifles Regiment to camp there. Do not distract the housemaids or gardeners with idle chit-chat. Under no circumstances are you to go near the Earl's hothouses or summer house – or speak or make eye contact with the Earl if you see him. The other cottage in the wall near the top of the gardens is The Bothy – where the under-gardeners and gamekeepers sleep. You can keep away from that too. While you are here, just… try and make yourself…useful." Each barked instruction chimed in time with Mrs Gilbert's thick stockinged ankles as she stomped up the wooden stairs. At the top, she turned. Her wide face was puce, the same colour as her work-worn housekeeper's fingers.

Clara tried to remember the barrage of words which had just been flung at her, but they flitted from her ears like moths and flew out of the door behind her.

"Are you listening, Clara? Shut the door behind you! Just like your father, always leaving them open."

"Yes, Aunt," Clara replied meekly, closing the door. Chinks of spades in soil, the laughter and chatter and busyness of the gardeners – all this was replaced with a silence which squeezed the air from Clara's lungs. The paper in her pocket pricked at her little finger, begging to be taken out and examined. Clara wondered if her aunt had truly gone, if she was finally alone, or if the woman was hovering there somewhere at the top of the stairs. "Later," she whispered under her breath to the paper. It didn't reply.

"You may call me Mrs Gilbert," Mrs Gilbert said in a voice so low it seemed to slither down the stairs and curl around Clara's feet like a snake.

Clara clenched her toes until they ached, wishing the snake would vanish.

"I'll show you your room," Mrs Gilbert said, her voice still sour, but less serpentine than before.

Pushing her secret deeper within the folds of her pocket, Clara gritted her teeth, picked up her small suitcase and followed Mrs Gilbert upstairs.

CHAPTER 2

The Boy

Sinking onto the lumpy bed, Clara took a deep breath. She thought of Father's back, straight as a rail, the shock of dark wavy hair that Mother was always trying to flatten. It seemed impossible that her father and *this* Mrs Gilbert were related – yet somehow, they were.

Father never spoke much of his older sister. But when he did, it was with fondness – stories of golden laughter-filled summers making tree houses and damming bubbling streams. Mrs Gilbert had greeted Clara three years ago with a warm hug and a punnet of ruby-red raspberries she had brought with her all the way from Suffolk. There had been no raspberries or a hug this time, just a stiff nod and a thin-lipped (and not at all generous) smile.

"Do you remember your Aunt Elizabeth who works for an earl in Suffolk? She and her husband will take you in for a while, until things are better here," Mother had said to Clara a few days before.

Clara had felt her face drop like a stone falling over a cliff. Over the past week Father's cough had worsened. Mother was often found sitting at his bedside, holding his hand. Sometimes when Clara walked past their bedroom door, their whispered conversations would halt. Her mother would click the door shut and Clara's heart would feel like it was curling into a tight knot. Father didn't like closed doors. "*Doors and windows are the key to a home's soul,*" he would say. "*If you are feeling sad, open them to release your melancholy. If you are feeling happy, open them to let the world embrace your joy.*" Doors and windows were always flung wide at home. Even in the middle of winter Father liked to breathe in the frosty morning air. Until the Great War. Until he got gas poisoning.

"It will only be for a short while," Mother had said, as she bent to stroke Neptune the cat. Neptune had purred and slinked around Mother's legs.

"A while," Clara had repeated. She had never been away from home before. And Suffolk must be very far away, for her aunt had not visited them for a long time. "But…what about school? I should stay here, help you look after Father. He is getting better, isn't he?"

Mother had lifted her head, given Clara a thin smile. "Father is going to stay in Devon. The air will be better there. He needs to convalesce. I am going too. It will only be for a short while," she had repeated. Then she had begun to prepare tea. The skin under her eyes was dark, like it had been smudged with dust from the coal pan. Clara longed to turn the dust into diamonds, to see her mother's eyes shine and laugh like they used to. But that hadn't happened since the day Clara didn't want to think about.

"Try not to worry, Clara. I will write to you whenever I can. Look on this as a little adventure. We will all be together again soon." When Mother said this last bit, her eyes had glazed over and the kettle had hissed and wobbled and boiled on the stove until Clara had picked up a dishcloth, lifted it off and placed it on the hotplate.

Clara shut the door on her memories and slid the envelope from her pocket. She lay it on the pillow beside her. Where to hide it? She remembered the scarecrows she had passed in the garden, stuffing spilling from their split coats. She examined her mattress. It was old, one of the seams coming loose on the underside. Clara carefully unpicked the thread, slid in the envelope, patted the mattress stuffing around it and let the blankets fall over it like a cloak.

Her envelope hidden, Clara stood up and greeted her new room. Father said it was always polite to say hello to your new surroundings. It used to make her giggle whenever they had visited somewhere new. "*Hello, museum. Thank you for having us,*" he would say as they walked through the enormous doors, Clara skipping beside him. "*Hello, paintings. Hello, statues. Hello, hello, hello.*"

Clara placed her hands on the rough whitewashed plaster of the attic room. "Hello, wall."

"Hello there," she said to a gnarly wooden table with a wobbly leg.

"Hello," she said, picking up a crocheted blanket folded on the end of her bed and holding it to her cheek. Clara thought about her bedroom at home, with its small wooden shelf filled with books, which was also home to her teddy bears and dolls (who were like old friends she could not bear to say goodbye to). She had not brought many things from home. Her worn copy of *The Jungle Book*. Some writing paper, a nib pen and a bottle of ink, so she could write to her mother and father. In her rush to pack she had forgotten to bring a teddy or a doll. A lump leaped to her throat as she thought about her stuffed friends sitting at home, waiting for her to return.

Her own house had only one flight of stairs and the bedrooms were so close together that the voices of her family were never far away. As the silence of the attic surrounded her, she had a strong sense that things would be different here.

Taking a deep breath, she looked up at the grainy attic beams and the ceiling (which slanted so steeply she could only stand upright in the centre of the room). "Oh, hello to you too," she said to a family of spindly spiders clinging to their webs between the oak-brown beams. Mother was scared of spiders and swatted at their webs with a feather duster until their gauzy patterns and hard work dissolved into nothing. Clara smiled. The spiders could stay. It would be nice to have some company in the eaves of this unfamiliar house.

She greeted the diamond-paned window last. Clara squeaked the glass clean with the edges of her apron, undid the catch and pushed it open. She took in a breath of early evening air, her eyes following the winding brick wall. The windows of the hothouses were dulling in the fading light. As she watched, the door of one opened outwards. A brief halo of steam, like dragon's breath, surrounded a boy. Clara leaned out of the window as far as she dared. His cap was pulled low over his face, but he looked about thirteen – maybe a year older than she was. Clara glanced around for the gardeners she had seen when she had arrived, but all was quiet aside for some crows ignoring the scarecrows and bravely pecking at the vegetable tops.

The boy was jumpy; he seemed like a hare about to bolt. He looked to his left and right. Then his eyes flicked upwards and met hers.

He froze.

Clara sucked in a breath and dipped down out of sight.

"Clara," Mrs Gilbert called. "Come and help me prepare tea." Her voice sounded quite cross, the same colour as her cheeks and fingers.

Clara stood up slowly and peered over the sill of the window. She blinked. The boy had gone, evaporated into the evening air just like the steam.

CHAPTER 3

Locked Door

Clara was being held down by a large grey-and-white husky dog, its fangs bared and ready to bite a chunk from her throat. "No," she squealed, batting the dog away. Its fur was wiry, not as soft as it looked. The dog bore down on her. "Get off, get away," she yelped. Her fingers clawed and grabbed and pinched.

"Stop it. Stop it, you silly, silly girl."

Clara jolted awake and sat up in bed.

Mrs Gilbert stood over Clara in the half-dark, funny little mouselike gasps coming from her mouth.

Clara's fingers were curled around something soft. Her dream sprang back at her. Unclenching her fist, her eyes widened. Wisps of grey dog's fur lay in her palm.

She touched them with a finger. They were thick and wiry.

Heavy footsteps thumped up the stairs. Mr Gilbert stood at the door in his nightshirt, his bare legs like a scrawny chicken's. "What in heaven's name?" he said, stepping into the room.

Clara looked from him, to the fur in her hand, to Mrs Gilbert. It was a triangle which made no sense.

"My...my...hair," Mrs Gilbert said, pointing a shaking finger at Clara's open palm. "I was trying to wake her and she...she grabbed me."

Oh, thought Clara. A wave of heat washed over her. Rain pattered against the glass of the open window as if in sympathy. "I'm sorry," Clara said limply. "I was having a nightmare...about a big...dog."

"A dog," Mr Gilbert said. He tilted his head and stared at Clara.

"It was...at my throat," Clara said, touching her neck gingerly, but there were no fang marks. She glanced down. There was no slash of crimson blood staining her nightdress.

"My hair," Mrs Gilbert squeaked again, patting at her head.

Clara held out the fuzz in her trembling hand. She

wasn't offering it to Mrs Gilbert. That would have been rude. But it wasn't hers to keep either.

Mrs Gilbert's slap was sharp and stinging.

The hair floated from Clara's hand to the floorboards like a falling cloud. Clara brought a hand to her cheek and thought of her father.

"*You are brave. And when you are brave, you can be anything you want to be,*" he would say to Clara when he tucked her up in bed.

"*Anything?*" she would reply eagerly.

"*A dog-sledding explorer travelling over snow-capped mountains, a hot-air balloonist soaring over scorched deserts, a botanist making fantastical discoveries in the Amazonian jungle, a doctor who can mend my poorly lungs. Just be brave, my Clara. Be brave.*" His eyes would go milky and far away then, like he wasn't sitting in Clara's sunny bedroom, but somewhere else entirely as he coughed and coughed, and Mother fussed and fussed with handkerchiefs and tinctures and cups of tea.

At school Clara would drink in everything the teacher said, like she was the thirstiest girl in the world, for Father said knowledge was the quickest way for Clara to achieve her dreams. But what he didn't know

23

was that many of the ideas he imagined for Clara's future gave her the occasional violent nightmare filled with sharp-toothed dogs, angry spitting camels and swamps so deep they swallowed her whole.

"Get dressed," Mrs Gilbert hissed. She pulled the window shut with a bang. "You can scrub the cottage floors while I'm at the Big House."

Mr Gilbert was rubbing his chin, like he was trying to remove a stubborn mark. His eyes were soft, like they were when she had arrived yesterday. He opened his mouth to speak. Clara held her breath. Was he going to defend her? But before he had the chance, Mrs Gilbert grabbed his arm and hustled him towards the door.

Clara sat rod-straight, her arms clasped around her knees. She strained her ears to hear Mr and Mrs Gilbert's whispers from the floor below. Only the odd word drifted up the stairs.

"…what's done is done…" (Mr Gilbert.)

"…harder than I thought…" (Mrs Gilbert.)

"…must do as her parents ask…" (Mr Gilbert.)

"…is it for the best?" (Mrs Gilbert.)

A tear slipped down Clara's sore cheek. She wiped it briskly with the edge of her sheet, which was worn in places but was clean and smelled of rose water. She had only been slapped once before in her life, by her mother after she had run into the road at the school gate and almost got bowled over by a horse and cart. Her mother's slap to the back of her legs had hurt, but it had been a well-deserved warning, like a bee sting. The cheek slap Mrs Gilbert had dispensed had been full of fiery intent.

The crocheted blanket on Clara's bed was like the garden outside her window, a patchwork of muted browns, earthy greens and dusky yellows. It was home-made, a muddle of dropped stitches in places. How could Mrs Gilbert's angry red fingers have made something so lovely? Clara reached down the side of the mattress to the gap in the stitching. The envelope was still there, but she wished with all her might it wasn't and that it was with its rightful owners. Pulling it out, she held it to her cheek and closed her eyes and tried her hardest not to think about home. As her mother said, this was just for a short while.

The water in the pail wobbled as Clara carried it up the stairs. She kneeled and began to scrub at the wooden floorboards on the landing outside Mr and Mrs Gilbert's bedroom. The chestnut-brown branches on the bottle-green wallpaper gave the effect of being in the woods on a gloomy winter's day and did nothing to lift her already low spirits. *Is this the type of adventure you thought I'd be having?* she asked her mother in her head. *Why is Mrs Gilbert so mean? She doesn't seem to like me one small bit.* But then again, she had accidentally pulled out a clump of Mrs Gilbert's hair, so maybe it wasn't surprising that, after a bad start, things had deteriorated even further.

Clara poked the door of Mr and Mrs Gilbert's bedroom open with the toe of her boot. "Hello, Mr and Mrs Gilbert's room," she said softly, laying a hand on a dark wooden dresser. When Mrs Gilbert last came to stay, Clara had been told to call her Aunt Elizabeth. Why could she not address her as Aunt now? Referring to her as Mrs Gilbert seemed odd and rather formal, like she was addressing a teacher at school. Her nose wrinkling, she stood at the window, watched the light dance on the small lake which formed a watery boundary to the southernmost edge of the gardens. Moorhens chattered in the reeds. Geese squabbled. Leaves from the trees whirled to the ground, drifted into the water and floated away like small boats on an exciting journey. It made her spirits lift a little.

On Mr and Mrs Gilbert's double bed lay another beautiful crocheted blanket. Except this one was duller than the one on her own bed, a cross-looking haze of greys and blacks. Clara was somehow not surprised that Mrs Gilbert did not like brightly coloured things.

When she had swept and scrubbed the floor, Clara slipped back onto the landing. There was a door next to the Gilberts' bedroom. Clara turned the brass knob. The door didn't open. It was locked. A frown pulled at her forehead. Mrs Gilbert had told her to scrub *all* of the floors in the cottage, hadn't she? She bent down and peered through the small keyhole. The room was decorated in the same dark-green wallpaper as the hallway. A wooden bureau sat under the window. On top of it lay a pile of papers. They looked like envelopes. A made-up bed stood against one wall. The fireplace was swept and laid. "Hello, little woodland room," Clara whispered.

"What are you doing?" Mrs Gilbert stood at the end of the landing in stockinged feet. Her cheeks were flushed and strands of hair were escaping from her cap.

"I was just…cleaning…like you asked," stammered Clara, standing up.

Mrs Gilbert's eyes were bright, like someone had lit

a fire behind them. "Leave that room alone, do you understand?" she whispered, taking a step towards Clara.

Clara took a step backwards and clutched at the wall. Was she going to be slapped again?

"I said, *do you understand*?" Mrs Gilbert repeated. Her eyes were grey as flint.

Clara nodded until she felt her head might wobble off and roll down the hall.

Mrs Gilbert glared at Clara, opened her bedroom door and slammed it so hard a small chunk of plaster fell from the wall and plopped onto the floorboard near Clara's feet. Clara picked it up and laid it in her palm. She gazed up at the place on the wall it had fallen from. A flap of wallpaper covering the plaster had come loose. Standing on tiptoes, she reached up and carefully peeled back its edge. Paper had been layered on paper. Underneath the woodland scene was the branch of a different tree, the curve of an orange mandarin and delicate white blossom. Clara chewed on her bottom lip. Why would anyone want to wallpaper over the beautiful spring walls and turn them into winter?

28

CHAPTER 4

Hothouse

The rap at the door of their small terraced house had come two days before Clara had been sent to stay with her aunt and uncle. Clara's mother had been busy tending to her father, so Clara had taken the letter from the post-boy with the blue cap and serious-looking eyes, telling him she would give it to her parents immediately. The sender's name and address were printed smartly in the bottom left corner: *War Office*.

Clara stared at the typeface now, wondering about the words waiting to be read inside. A hard lump of guilt lodged in her chest. She hadn't meant to hide it. She had slipped it into her pocket just until Father's cough settled. Just until Mother's eyes looked a little brighter. But it hadn't and they hadn't and now she had been sent away and it was too late to do anything about it. She had intended to give it to Mrs Gilbert...but after the slap, the thought of explaining the circumstances in which she had taken the envelope (and Mrs Gilbert's possible reaction) made her stomach wobble. Perhaps her only option was to wait a little, return it to Mother and Father in person. Mother had said that she would only be with the Gilberts for a short while. But what if waiting a few days made matters even worse? What if the news inside was so important they needed to know immediately?

Clara blew out the candle on her window sill with a heavy sigh, rested her chin in her hands and looked out over the gardens. Her skin burned with guilt as she watched the moon, low and shiny and bathing everything in a shimmery blue light. She imagined her guilt and confusion floating out into the blackness with the spiralling candle smoke. Her mind was whirring, going around and around like a train on a circular track.

A soldier in a smart green uniform striding down a terraced street.

A fistful of hair.

A dog with bared teeth looming over her.

A locked woodland room.

The envelope.

Clara sucked in breath after breath of chilly air.

Boom!

Rat-tat-tat-tat!

Clara grasped the window sill, her heart hammering against her ribs in time to the sudden sound of gunfire.

Rat-tat-tat-tat-tat!

Boom-boom!

Boom-boom-boom!

It must be the Rifles Regiment on a night exercise. Mr Gilbert had told her (over boiled eggs at breakfast that morning) that many of the Regiment's highly skilled gunners had been killed at the Second Battle of Ypres the year before. Some of those men had worked for the Earl and he had been devastated by the losses. Determined to do his bit for the war effort, he was allowing a hundred of the Regiment's new soldiers to camp and train on his land. Mr Gilbert had leaned across the table and told Clara softly she should prepare herself for the sound of rifles being fired long into each night, as the Regiment prepared to move out to France, perhaps to the Somme battlefields.

As Mr Gilbert spoke, Clara had thought of Father's

daily newspaper, brimming with news about the Battle of the Somme. The early reports had been positive, told of few casualties and many successes. But Clara's father had shaken his head and said the reality was quite different and that she shouldn't believe all she read. If her father was right, that meant there was a chance some of the new soldiers camping and training on the Earl's estate would not return. She had placed her spoon down, her appetite for breakfast suddenly gone.

Startled by the rifle fire, a flock of birds roosting in the trees whirled into the air. They looked like mystical winged creatures as they squawked across the planting beds. The mute scarecrows listened and watched, straw heads tilted in surprise. Someone else was watching too, his head tipped to the spectacle overhead. Clara squinted. The boy! He was sitting with his back to a low wall opposite the hothouses. The birds disappeared, and the boy turned his attention to something lying in his lap. It was too dark and she was too far away to see what it was. The boy hunched over, giving it his full attention. Suddenly he stood up, pushed whatever he had been looking at into his jacket pocket and disappeared.

Clara blinked, leaning out of the window as far as

she dared. The still air folded around her like a blanket. How could he have vanished again? Was he a ghost? A magician? His head bobbed up and he reappeared. Clara rubbed her eyes.

The boy shook out a blanket in the way you might shake out a dusty rug. He spread it on the grass and lay down, turning his face to the blue moon as if it was the sun bathing him in warmth. Clara watched him as the *booms* and *rat-a-tats* echoed on, deeper into the woods now. She was watching him like a spy. It felt wrong, but she could not tear her eyes away. Clara watched and watched until her eyes grew leaden and started to close.

Climbing back into bed, she pulled her own blanket tight around her shoulders. There was something intriguing about the boy that made her want to find out who he was. She listened to the far away *rat-tat-tats* and *booms* until she drifted into an uneasy sleep full of gunfire and soldiers, her mother and father, unopened letters and locked doors and a boy who liked to lie under a moon masquerading as the sun.

"Under no circumstances are you to go near the Earl's hothouses." Mrs Gilbert's voice echoed in Clara's head

the next morning, as she slinked around the perimeter of the hothouse where she had last seen the boy. She saw the stooped shoulders of Mr Gilbert and several of the other gardeners as they pulled up parsnips from the planting beds on the other side of the garden. A man was sitting having a smoke near the fruit trees, a white-and-brown spaniel curled at his feet.

Clara pressed a hand to one of the glass panes. It was damp. She drew a small circle, with dotted eyes and a nose and a smiling mouth. She bumped her fingers along the windows until she turned a corner and came to the entrance of the hothouse. Near it was the stump of a felled tree, the bark furry with moss. Clara skirted around it and down the five stone steps which led to the door. Her breaths came a little faster. She brought a hand to the cheek Mrs Gilbert had slapped. It still smarted when she pressed on it.

She tentatively gave the door a push and it swung open with a creak. A wall of soupy warm air hit her in the face. She drew in a breath. She drew in another and the tightness in her neck began to dissolve. The boy wasn't there. Of course he wasn't. He only appeared at night, like a fox or a badger.

She blinked at the two raised planting beds in front

of her. Thick metal pipes rose from the ground and travelled under the length of the beds. One of the pipes near her feet gurgled. She bent down and touched it. "Ouch." She pulled her thumb away from the heat and sucked at it.

On top of the planting beds sat pots containing spiky oval fruit within crowns of long sharp-looking leaves. *Pineapples!* Clara smiled and walked down one of the planting rows, past a bench of gardening equipment – metal watering cans, a wicker basket, a small trowel and fork.

As she neared the end of the hothouse the pineapples grew larger and larger. They were like the matryoshka dolls she had received in her Christmas stocking one year.

"*You know they are supposed to sit inside one another, don't you?*" Mother had said with an amused smile.

"*But I feel sorry for the smaller ones. They don't want to be in the dark,*" Clara had replied, lining them up in a row on her window ledge.

Clara bent down and pressed her thumb onto the hard, spiky husk of one of the pineapples. "Hello, fruit," she said softly.

For Clara, pineapple was a treat. She had often seen

whole ones for sale at the fruiterers, but the only pineapple she had tasted had been canned, so sweetened and swimming in syrup that the yellow flesh had made her teeth ache. Last year one of her mother's friends had rented a home-grown pineapple as a centrepiece for her son's wedding party. Clara had circled around it, *ooh*ing and *aah*ing with everyone else. It was as if they were viewing a precious monument in a museum. "It cost me a week's pay to rent this," her mother's friend had said proudly. To rent a beautiful fruit and not be able to taste it seemed like the stupidest thing in the world to Clara. When the wedding party had moved into the garden for some raucous (and out of tune) singing and dancing, Clara crept back into the dining room and stood in front of the pineapple. She had reached across and touched one of its spikes. The sudden urge to pick the pineapple up, take a knife to it, chop its flesh into tiny pieces and nibble on it had been overwhelming.

The very same urge was filling her now. She pushed her fingers deep into her apron pockets (Mother had packed her three pinafore aprons, instructing that one should be worn each day to protect her day dresses from the outdoors) and felt the tip of the envelope.

She sighed, pulled it out and sank to the floor, her dress skirts and apron puffing around her like a mushroom. She nibbled on a fingernail. Should she open it? It wasn't one of the feared pink telegrams that Mrs Buxton over the road had received to inform her of the death of her son. The poor woman had taken to her bed and four months later was still in it, her bedroom curtains tightly drawn. But surely letters from the War Office could only mean one of two things: injury or death? Finding out the truth would change everything. Was she ready for the truth? Were any of them?

Heavy feet thumped down the steps to the hothouse. There was a muffled cough at the doorway.

Clara scrabbled to her feet and pushed the envelope back into her pocket. Curling her nails into her palms, she held her breath as the door to the hothouse swung open and a flood of fresh air rushed down the steps.

CHAPTER 5

Milky-eyed Man

A young man wearing a gardening jacket with a mustard-yellow lining stared at Clara from the top of the hothouse steps, his forehead as furrowed as the newly seeded planting beds outside. He pushed his round spectacles up his nose as Clara continued to hold her breath, waiting for the telling-off which was surely about to come.

"What are you doing in here?" he asked.

Clara racked her brains for something sensible to say. Should she say she had been cold and had come inside for the warmth? Yet it was warm outside, the October sun emitting a welcome glow that in a few weeks would be gone. Maybe she should say she had been passing and heard a noise and came in to investigate? Or she could just tell him the truth – that she had been curious as to why Mrs Gilbert was so adamant she should not go near the hothouses.

"I was…curious," Clara said eventually.

His eyes narrowed. Clara saw that the lens of his left eye was covered in a milky film. The young man walked towards her. "You're Alfred's niece, aren't you?"

"Alfred?" Clara said in confusion, trying not to stare at the man's cloudy eye.

"Mr Gilbert?"

"Oh, yes," Clara said, a flush rising up her neck like a vine.

Now the man was closer, Clara saw he was barely a man at all, maybe sixteen or seventeen.

He leaned on the workbench. "I guess being curious is as good a reason as any. I'm Robert, one of the under-gardeners. And you are…?"

"Clara," she replied with a shy smile. "Um…I hope you don't mind me asking, but what's an under-gardener?"

Robert smiled and picked up a metal trowel from the bench. "I suppose I'm an assistant to Mr Gilbert. I know this and that about plants and equipment.

Though there are plenty of others better at gardening than me. If I'm honest, all the ins-and-outs of it can get a bit confusing sometimes."

"Yes, I imagine it must," said Clara.

"So…what do you make of the hothouses? The Earl's pride and joy they are," Robert said, jabbing at the soil around one of the plants with the trowel.

"They are lovely. The plants are…so different to what is grown outside," Clara said.

Robert looked up. "The Earl is a collector of tropical plants. I think he imagines himself to be an explorer – although he doesn't find these plants himself. He sends people overseas to do that."

"Does he visit these hothouses often then?" Clara asked, glancing at the door. It would not do at all for the Earl to catch her in there. Imagining Mrs Gilbert's reaction made her clutch onto the edge of the planting bench.

"Not any more." Robert placed the trowel down, reached across and stroked one of the pineapple leaves. "You'll more often find him sitting in the summer house now."

"The summer house?" said Clara.

Robert jerked a thumb over his shoulder, towards the door. "It overlooks the lake. A small brick building with big windows and doors. It's heated, just like these hothouses, but it's not for growing plants. The Earl and his family use it for entertaining their guests, or as a place to sit on a fair day."

"But how sad that the Earl doesn't come and see his own plants. To have someone collect and grow them for you, but not to visit them," Clara said.

Robert smiled, then his expression became dreamy and faraway. "I would like to visit where these pineapples are grown. Sometimes I come in here and imagine beaches with silky sand, azure-blue seas that are as warm as a bath, filled with rainbow-coloured fishes and coral." He sighed heavily, like a weight was attached to his shoulders. "Not much chance of that with a war on though."

Robert sounded like her father. She wished he would carry on talking, but he was silent now, his head bowed as he sieved the soil through his fingers.

"Is your father at war?" Robert asked suddenly.

Clara's shoulders stiffened. "He was," she replied. *A soldier in uniform. Marching.* She stamped on the thoughts before they took control of her lungs and made it difficult to breathe.

The warm air was thick with silence.

Robert's fingers stilled. He looked up. "He came back then?"

Clara nodded.

"I'm mostly blind in my left eye – I was born like it. I wouldn't pass the medical exam if I tried to enlist in the army," he said. His head was bowed again but Clara thought his cheeks were a little redder than before. "Five of Mr Gilbert's gardeners have been conscripted. Means lots more work for the rest of us. There's even talk of women from the village coming to help, as there are so few men." Robert patted the soil around the base of one of the pineapple plants. "But I'm doing my bit. Today I took a cart of vegetables and fruit from the garden to the military hospital. We'll be sending four carts a week from now on. The Earl says we must help the war effort."

An idea was bubbling at the edges of Clara's brain. *Make yourself useful,* Mrs Gilbert had said when she arrived. "Could I…help?" Clara asked quietly.

"Help?" said Robert.

"In the gardens. I could…pick apples, or pull vegetables, or something. For the hospital."

Robert smiled. "Know much about gardening, do you?"

Clara felt the flush in her already hot cheeks deepen. "I could learn."

42

Robert's good eye was thoughtful. "We are short of gardeners." He tapped a finger on his chin. "Let me talk to your uncle."

Clara smiled her thanks and turned to leave. "Oh, the boy who works in the gardens. Who is he?"

Robert stood up, brushed the dirt from his palms. "A boy?" A frown puckered his forehead. He took a step towards her. "The only boy who works here is Red the hall boy."

"Hall boy?"

"You really don't know how this place works, do you?" said Robert in an amused voice. "Red stokes the boilers, polishes shoes, does the jobs no one else wants to do and earns a pittance for it too."

"And he's called Red?" Clara said, scrunching her nose.

"On account of his hair," Robert said with a grin.

The boy Clara had seen in the gardens at night had not got red hair, she was sure of it.

"What did this boy look like?" asked Robert, his head tilted.

"It must have been my eyes playing tricks. Sometimes I get…nightmares," she said lightly, hoping that Robert didn't pick up the waver in her voice.

"Hmm," said Robert, pushing his hands into his pockets.

At the door, Clara turned. "Please don't tell Mrs Gilbert I was in here. She asked me…to keep away from the hothouses."

A flash of something crossed Robert's face. It was too lightning-quick for Clara to decipher what it meant. "Your secret is safe with me," he said.

Throwing him a quick smile, Clara pushed through the door, ran up the stone steps and out into the breezy sunshine.

"Oh, and Clara."

Clara turned.

Robert was standing in the doorway. He pushed his spectacles further up his nose again. "If you do happen across this boy another time, and he turns out not to be one of your nightmares, be sure to let me know."

Clara stared at him for a second, then gave him a brief nod. Robert did not believe the boy was a figment of her imagination, that much was clear. But something told Clara that she needed to keep this boy a secret from Robert – and everyone else – until she found out exactly who he was and what he was doing in the Earl's gardens.

CHAPTER 6

Search for the Boy

How is it possible for time to pass so slowly? mused Clara as she lay on her back in the midst of a swathe of thigh-high wild flowers near the east wall of the gardens. She pulled out a blade of long grass and tried to whistle with it. A low-level screech was all she managed. She sighed and let the grass fall from her fingers.

She had been with the Gilberts for five days (which at that point felt more like five months). There was no school or lessons to keep up with. There was no daily drill in the yard with Mrs Philpott, who back at St Michael's School would make the girls march endlessly on the spot (while the boys had a much more interesting time being taught how to box). There was no catching up with friends over school lunches (although Clara had to admit she far preferred the Gilberts' freshly baked loaves, game pies and tongue-tingling pickles to the school's stodgy bread-and-dripping). As a consequence, her days had already lost their structure and stretched endlessly onwards. It was as if someone had stolen all of her purpose and hidden it just out of sight over the horizon.

She had spent the last few days searching the gardens for the boy she had seen from the attic window. She roamed the centre of the gardens, peeping through the steamy hothouse windows when no one else was around. She had wound her way through the sweet-smelling apple and pear trees, which grew in neat lines along the south-facing walls. She explored the unkept area of the gardens along the eastern wall, a combination of volcano-like compost heaps, the odd pile of rubble and sprouting wild flowers and nettles. But the boy was nowhere. Maybe he *had* been a vision in one of her nightmares?

She had seen Robert a few times in the gardens. She watched him and the other under-gardeners from a distance, plucking apples from the trees or pushing barrow-loads of vegetable peelings from the Big House down to the compost heaps. The work did not look difficult, but it looked busy, and busy was what she was desperate for.

Once or twice Robert had given her a friendly wave and shouted hello, but he had not come over to chat – or to tell her that Mr Gilbert had agreed to Clara helping in the gardens. The endless free time allowed thoughts of missing home and Mother and Father to creep into her head. She pulled out the envelope from her apron pocket and held it to the sky until it covered the sun. *No. This will not do at all.* The thoughts of what it might say were horrid and must not be allowed to take hold.

"You rotter! Give me back my net, Constance," called a chirpy voice.

Clara sat up in a rush, pushing the envelope back into her pocket. Two small girls, maybe seven or eight – both in green dresses with dandelion-yellow sashes, which Clara very much admired – were running across the gardens towards her. The smaller of the two girls was waving two butterfly nets in the air and giggling.

Clara picked up her straw boater (which Mrs Gilbert insisted she carry everywhere with her) and jammed it onto her head.

"Greta, please take control of the girls. It will not do, having them running around on such a warm day and spoiling their dresses. Take them to the summer house for refreshments," called a slim lady carrying a lace-edged parasol.

Clara saw that another lady was following the first. She was wearing a beige dress with a brown sash. A funny round hat, a little like a biscuit, sat on her severely pulled-back hair. She had seen ladies in similar uniforms pushing prams with sleeping (or sometimes crying) babies in the park at home. She must be the girls' nanny.

"Look, Mother. A girl hiding in the weeds," said the girl carrying the nets. The ladies stopped and stared in Clara's direction.

Clara felt warmth spread up her neck and spill onto her cheeks. She was not hiding, she was just…well, not doing much of anything really.

The slim lady whispered to the nanny, who was giving Clara a hard and disapproving stare.

Oh dear, thought Clara. What should she do? Should she stand up and tell them she was the Gilberts' niece. She did not want them to think she was trespassing. But then again, if they were from the Big House, would they even know who the Gilberts were? The other day Mrs Gilbert had said (with a haughty sniff) that she prided herself on being able to undertake her job as housekeeper without being seen or heard by the Earl and his family.

Clara smoothed the wrinkles from her apron and was about to stand up and present herself (deciding it would be ruder not to) when, with a swing of her lacy parasol, the lady turned on her heel and walked away. The nanny quickly gathered up the two gawking girls, like a mother duck rounding up its ducklings, and hurried them off in the direction of the summer house.

Clara lowered herself down to the ground, her boater slipping off her head. She brought her hands to her warm cheeks and breathed in the scent of flowers and soil and fresh air, which soothed away some of her embarrassment. The Earl's family had more structure to their days than she had – even if it was centred on looking after their dresses and catching poor unsuspecting butterflies. Something had to change soon, or else she felt she might go ever so slightly mad. Perhaps solving the mystery of the elusive boy once and for all would keep her mind occupied until she was sent back home.

CHAPTER 7

Homesick

After a tea of fresh bread, crumbly cheddar cheese and an assortment of ochre and russet-red pickles (Mr Gilbert telling Clara with a seed of pride in his voice that pickling the garden's produce was a small way they could ensure the vegetables stretched as far as possible in a time of war), the Gilberts went to sit in the small parlour which had a view of the Earl's lake.

Clara dried the last of the dishes, wiped her hands on the tea towel and followed them. She hovered at the door. Mrs Gilbert's fingers were busy knitting with a ball of inky-blue wool. The days might be warm, but the evenings were threaded with an autumn chill and Mr Gilbert had lit a small fire before tea. He sat in front

of it, scribbling in a small notebook.

Clara pushed her hands into her apron pockets. "I just wondered…if any letters from Mother have arrived for me?" she asked. Her mother had said she would write often to update Clara on Father's health. To Clara that meant every day. Yet each day when she asked Mrs Gilbert if any letters had arrived, there were none. Surely Mother would have found time by now to put her thoughts on paper, and locate an envelope and a pillar-red postbox to slip them in? She imagined Mother and Father taking evening strolls along a blustery seafront, seagulls wheeling in the air, Father clutching a newspaper cone of fat chips heavily coated in salt. A wave of homesickness sat on her shoulders like a heavy black cloak as she waited for Mrs Gilbert's answer.

"No," said Mrs Gilbert. Her fingers expertly twisted the knitting needles; in and out and around and up and down went the dark wool.

The pockets of Clara's homesickness cloak filled with rocks.

Mr Gilbert looked up. "Come and sit a while, child," he said, giving her a warm smile.

Clara's breath hitched in her throat. She entered the room gingerly, as if she was treading on glass.

There were only two high-backed wooden chairs in the room, and they were both taken. She had not been in the parlour before, except to clean the floors. Every evening after tea she returned to her attic room to read about Mowgli and Baloo's adventures in *The Jungle Book*, or to stare out of the window, hoping for another sight of the mysterious boy who she hadn't seen for the past three days. Where should she sit? On the rug in front of the fire? Clara thought of Neptune, the way he would curl up on Clara's lap like smoke and purr into the flames. He was being looked after by a neighbour, and must be wondering what had happened to his family, who had all disappeared, one after the other.

The fire crackled and the smell of woodsmoke tickled Clara's throat as she lowered herself to the rug, hugging her knees to her chest.

Mr Gilbert coughed a ragged cough.

Click-click went Mrs Gilbert's knitting needles.

The noises and smells should have been soothing, but Clara found them stifling.

"However, I did receive news from your mother yesterday," Mrs Gilbert said. She placed her knitting on her lap and pulled at the lace collar of her blouse, as if it was too tight around her neck. "You will be here longer than we first thought."

Clara forced her mouth to stay closed, when all it wanted to do was drop open.

Mr Gilbert's pencil paused.

Mrs Gilbert picked up the needles again and continued twisting them through the wool.

Clara clasped her own hands together to stop them from shaking. "Is it because of Father? Can I read Mother's letter? Please?" she asked under her breath.

Mrs Gilbert seemed not to have heard her. Her fingers wound the wool this way and that, having a conversation all of their own.

Mr Gilbert glanced at Mrs Gilbert, then looked away at the fire.

"But what about school?" said Clara anxiously. "If I stay here longer I will fall behind and—"

"You will catch up soon enough when you return home," Mrs Gilbert interrupted. "I must say that I feel school is rather a luxury in these difficult times." She reached up to touch her gold necklace with its delicate cross that nestled at the base of her throat. She gave Mr Gilbert a quick glance, but he was not looking at his wife. His eyes were focused on the words in his notebook that were too far away for Clara to read.

Words rose inside Clara's head like lava in a volcano. *I don't want to get behind at school. Why won't you let me read my mother's letter? What are you hiding from me? Is Father getting sicker?* Her lips quivered with the effort of keeping the words inside.

Mrs Gilbert cleared her throat. "Is there anything else?"

"Yes," Clara found herself saying breathlessly. Her lips seemed to be disconnected from her brain, moving by themselves. "I met Robert a few days ago, one of the under-gardeners. He said he would ask…if I could help gather fruit and vegetables for the military hospital. If I'm not to be at school, then it's important I do my bit, isn't it?"

Mr Gilbert looked at Mrs Gilbert.

Mrs Gilbert looked at her knitting needles.

Clara held her breath.

"No," Mrs Gilbert said curtly.

Mr Gilbert was chewing on the end of his pencil and staring into the fire again.

"But…" said Clara, her voice wavering. Was there to be no explanation, no reason for this decision?

"I said no," Mrs Gilbert said in a low voice. "Make

yourself useful indoors. You can clean the windows tomorrow."

"Now, Lizzy…" said Mr Gilbert in a soft voice, laying down his pencil and leaning forwards in his chair. "Clara could be a help. Cook's sent down an extra-long list of produce she needs for meals at the Big House. And there is much to pick and collect for the hospital deliveries. We are so short of men…"

"I said no," Mrs Gilbert said again, staring at her lap.

Clara didn't remember how she got into the hall. She did not know whether it was Mr or Mrs Gilbert who shut the parlour door behind her.

Hushed voices came from within.

"Tell her…" (Mr Gilbert.)

"How will telling her possibly help matters?" (Mrs Gilbert.)

"It may help her understand…" (Mr Gilbert.)

Clara heard Mrs Gilbert's needles and fingers whispering over the wool, like they were trying to twist their secrets into its folds. Numbness climbed Clara's spine. She opened the door to the gardens and half-fell out onto the step. She pulled in a breath of cool night air, and another and another, until her skin was less tight.

Things were piling up on Clara, like in a game of cards. She turned them over one by one. A boy only seen at night. Mr and Mrs Gilbert's whispered conversations. Mrs Gilbert's permanent crossness and her refusal to let Clara read her mother's letter. She thought of the jigsaws Father and Mother would buy at Christmas, the family arguments over which they should choose – steam trains or aeroplanes or idyllic wintry village scenes of children building carrot-nosed and coal-eyed snowmen. What would they make of *this* puzzle?

Clara pressed her lips together. Mother and Father weren't there. They were in Devon and she knew she mustn't bother them with things like strange boys and conversations not meant for her ears. But all the same, things were happening which needed answers.

At that moment, there was a scuffle in the gardens, just out of sight beyond the edge of the light spilling from the door. A fox, or something else? *Someone* else? Clara took a deep breath and stepped into the dark, her heart thumping hard against her ribs. It was time to start putting the pieces of this puzzle together.

CHAPTER 8

The Mandarin

Clara had never thought of herself as particularly brave. When she was ten, her friend Elsa had fallen into a well. They had been throwing in pebbles, and in her usual overenthusiastic way, Elsa had thrown herself over the low wall along with a particularly large stone. Clara had frozen as she heard the plop of the stone, followed by a larger and meatier splash as her friend hit the icy water head-first. The thoughts that went through Clara's head were precisely these:

I must be brave.

I must rescue her.

These thoughts went through Clara's head several times, but to her extreme annoyance her body refused to translate the thoughts into actions, and all her fingers did was clench and unclench. Clench and unclench. Clara's body was still frozen when, having heard Elsa's high-pitched wails, Phillip King arrived with a large stick and pulled Elsa out like an overwrought fish, arms flailing and goosebumped skin dripping. Clara had taken off her jumper and wrapped it around Elsa, soothed her, told her everything would be fine and hurried her home to her anxious mother and a warm bath.

Clara's fingers had still been clenching and unclenching when her father came to say goodnight that evening. He had placed his hands over hers. His grip was firm and steadying.

"What if Elsa had drowned because of what I didn't do?" Clara had whispered tearfully.

Mother's soft, familiar laugh had drifted up the stairs. It wrapped around Clara's body like silk.

Father had looped an arm around Clara's shoulder and kissed her twice on the head. He smelled of pipe smoke and the ginger pudding Mother had made for tea. Clara had closed her eyes and let her body relax into his side. "Sometimes pretending to be brave is enough," he had said wearily. "Something we must all try hard at while there's a war on, especially now that I've enlisted in the army and may soon be going away."

Long after the sun had said goodbye for another day and her parents had retired to bed, Clara thought about what her father had said. She twisted the words this way and that way, but they still did not make sense. For she hadn't pretended to be brave when Elsa had fallen into the well. She hadn't pretended anything at all. She turned over in her head the discussions her mother and father had most evenings after tea, about whether her mother should take a job at the local munitions factory. Her father said it was perilous work. Aside from the risks of poisoning (or turning yellow from exposure to the chemicals), there were also terrible tales of factory explosions and high death tolls. But her mother shrugged those issues aside, and said she was determined to do her bit until the day peace was declared, if that day ever came. Her mother was brave. Her father had said so. It was only Clara who was not brave.

The darkness of the gardens enveloped Clara like velvet. There was no blue moon. No *rat-a-tat* of rifles firing in the woods or startled birds cawing overhead tonight. The gardens were silent and still, as if they were watching Clara, waiting to see what she would do next. She thought of Father's advice. *Sometimes pretending to be brave is enough.* She took a deep breath of soft garden air, her feet treading quietly on the grassy paths past the sleeping tumbledown scarecrows, past the orchard of fruit trees…

Then a noise, the scuff of a boot on a paving slab to her right.

She paused, tilted her head and listened.

Another scuffle. The creak of a door. Clara crouched beside the hothouse where she now found herself, imagining herself as small as the tiniest of her matryoshka dolls. She glanced behind her. She was in the middle of the gardens now, hidden from anyone who might be watching from the cottage, hidden from the fruit trees where some of the men liked to sit with their backs to the trunks, having an evening smoke.

The skin on Clara's shoulders tightened.

There was the sound of footsteps running lightly across grass.

Clara strained her ears until she could hear them no more. Standing up, she quickly walked the length of the hothouse until she came to the spot where she had seen the boy before. But there was no blanket laid out on the grass, no boy with a cap pulled low over his face. She skirted around the old tree stump, then paused, her breath hitching in her throat. There, in the centre of the stump was a single perfect mandarin, one green waxy leaf clinging to its short stalk. Clara stared into the dark. Heard the hoot of an owl. A fleeting smell drifted under her nose, something like pipe smoke. She bent down and picked the fruit up, cradled it in her palms, gave it a sniff. It reminded her of Christmas, of laughter and games around the fire. This fruit didn't belong on a mossy tree stump. So why had it been left there? And by whom?

A burst of raindrops tapped on the glass of the nearby hothouse like fingernails as Clara peered into the gloom. Had it been left for someone else? Perhaps she should look after it, for surely it would get spoilt sitting here in the rain. Picking up the mandarin, she put it in her pocket, then wiped her cheeks. She glanced back in the direction of the cottage and her bedroom window. She would be soaked by the time she had run across the grass. She imagined Mrs Gilbert's sour face at the sight of Clara's sodden hair, her damp skirts and apron.

Clara darted down the steps to the hothouse which

stood a short distance behind the one she had been in before, her fingers lingering on the brass doorknob. The door was slightly ajar. Pushing it open, she tentatively stepped inside, breathing in the sweet warmth. The sound of the rain was thunderous as her eyes slowly adjusted to the dark shapes in front of her. It was not at all like the pineapple hothouse. This was like being in an orchard covered by a crystal cloak. Larger trees were trained to lengths of wooden trellis that were attached to posts between the glass panes. Clara reached up and touched a globe of fruit dangling from a branch. It was soft and furry. A peach. Smaller trees in cauldron-sized pots were scattered along the gravel planting beds, heavy with waxy lemons, mandarins and limes. She smiled as the glass panes rattled and hummed in the rain.

"Hello, lime tree," she whispered, holding a glossy leaf between her finger and thumb.

"Hello," whispered a voice ahead of her.

Clara's skin flashed hot and cold at the same time. Someone was inside the hothouse. She was being watched.

She peered into the darkness and saw the dim outline of a person half-hidden behind one of the larger peach trees. The figure stepped out from behind the branches.

Clara automatically took a step backwards, and then another towards the door.

"Hello," whispered the voice again.

Perhaps it was finally the boy she had been searching for... But with this thought, Clara's boot heel clipped something, which fell over with a metallic clatter. Stumbling, she tripped backwards into one of the smaller trees and landed on the concrete floor with a thump. *Oh cripes,* she thought, as the person walked towards her. Caught again in the Earl's hothouses. She dragged in a breath and looked up at the figure, her eyes widening in surprise.

CHAPTER 9

Will

"Golly. Are you alright?" It was a boy. *The Boy.*

"I'm fine," whispered Clara, even though her head was aching, and her palms were scuffed and gritty from her fall.

The boy was holding out a hand to her. Even in the dull light, Clara could see that it was a dirty hand, nails blackened as if they had been dipped in a pot of ink.

Ignoring him, she pushed herself up and examined her own pockmarked hands.

The boy bent down to the scattering of soil, a few leaves and two small limes that had been dislodged by Clara's fall. He scooped the limes into his hand, his forehead crinkling.

"Is…is the tree damaged?" Clara whispered. Just a minute before she had been saying hello to the lovely tree and now it was broken.

"It will live," the boy whispered back. "I'm sorry. It was my fault, startling you like that." Without warning he clapped a hand to his mouth and smothered a rasping cough.

"No, I shouldn't have been in here. It was raining and I just came in for a second to shelter." Words bubbled from Clara's mouth like a stream racing downhill.

The boy flashed her a quick smile as he placed the fallen limes next to the pot the tree was growing in. He coughed again, smothering the sound with the crook of his arm. Then after he had swept up the soil with his hands and tipped it back into the pot, he reached into his jacket pocket and pulled out a small notebook. Flipping it open, he carefully slipped the fallen leaves inside. *How very odd*, thought Clara. As he returned the book to his pocket, something fell to the ground.

Clara bent over and picked it up. It was a long, thin leaf which had been folded like a concertina. She handed it to him.

"It's from a pineapple plant," said the boy. "I draw

them – the plants and leaves, I mean. It's what I do, when I'm not stoking the boiler to heat these hothouses." He pushed the folded leaf into his pocket.

Clara remembered what Robert had said and squinted at the boy's hair, but it was hidden under his cap. "So… you're the hall boy? You work at the Big House?"

The boy let out a small laugh. It was bright, like silver. "No. Not quite. I'm just Will."

Clara smiled. "Oh. Hello, 'just Will'. I'm Clara."

Will held out his hand again. "Nice to meet you," he said, giving her a funny half-bow, which made Clara want to giggle. This time she reached out and shook his hand. His grasp was firm and warm and stung her grazed palms, but she found she did not mind one bit.

Reaching into her pocket, she pulled out the mandarin she had found on the tree stump. "I found this in the gardens."

Will took a step closer and peered at it. "That's curious. I found a mandarin by the lake the other night, near the reeds."

"That *is* curious," said Clara, wrinkling her nose. "What should I do with it?"

Will shrugged. "Eat it. Someone must have dropped it."

Clara pushed the mandarin back into her pocket and gave him a quick smile. "You said you stoke the boiler. Is it in here?" she asked, looking around.

"No. It's underground, behind the Earl's summer house," Will replied.

Clara remembered the way Will had disappeared into thin air as she was watching him from her bedroom window. An underground room. Maybe that explained it.

The dull *rat-tat-tat-tat* of rifle fire echoed off the glass walls of the hothouse, making Clara jump. She folded her arms against her pounding heart.

"It's just the Regiment," Will said. "You'll hear them practising every night. There's nothing to be afraid of."

Clara very much doubted she would ever get used to the sound of rifles being fired night after night. The thought of the Regiment roaming the Earl's woods and fields in the dark made her shiver with unease. But Will was right. She must try and get used it, even if it did remind her of things she would rather forget.

"I'm afraid I'm going to have to ask you to do me a tremendous favour," Will said, taking off his cap and holding it in his hands. A lock of wavy dark hair rolled into his left eye. He pushed it behind his ear.

"My…a…friend got me this job. You see, the thing is, my mother and father are gone and I have nowhere else to go." Will jammed his cap back on his head. It was so low now that Clara could barely see his eyes. Maybe that was the point.

"My goodness. How terribly sad," Clara replied. She pushed a hand into her pocket and felt the tip of the envelope there, where she always kept it. "When you say they are gone…"

Will's lips pressed together in a string-thin line. "Mother died when I was a baby. Father died on the Front a month ago."

Clara swallowed the peach-sized lump which had jumped into her throat. Her father had damaged lungs, but at least he had returned home. She thought of all those other men who were giving up their lives for their country, leaving behind loved ones whose lives would be tumbled upside down and inside out by the horror of it all.

"I stoke the boilers day and night and must keep out of sight. My friend says the Earl – and Mr Gilbert the head gardener – mustn't find out about me," Will said quietly. "Are you any good at keeping secrets?"

Clara gave him a small smile. "Actually, I think I am rather good at that."

Will gave her a nod as if he had expected nothing less. He gulped back another cough, his shoulders shaking with the effort.

"You should be careful though. I saw you from my window," Clara said. "And that cough…sounds awful."

"I know you saw me," Will said simply. "The boiler's been making odd noises. I went to check the thermometers in the hothouses. You were watching from Gardener's Cottage." It was a statement, not a question. "And my cough is rather beastly. It's just… dusty in the boiler house, is all."

The patter of the rain was lessening.

"I should go," Clara said uneasily. "The Gilberts are my aunt and uncle. They might be wondering where I am."

The hard line of Will's jaw seemed to suggest that he knew exactly who Mr and Mrs Gilbert were and was under no illusion about whether they would have noticed if Clara was snugly tucked up in her bed or not.

"I am staying with them because my father is ill. He and my mother are in Devon, so he can convalesce," Clara said. "But so far, it's not quite the visit I thought it would be."

Will nodded as if he understood. Clara wondered if

he had heard Mrs Gilbert's shrieks through the open window as Clara had grabbed a fistful of her hair.

"Do you think…maybe…you'll visit the gardens again…at night?" Will asked quietly, pushing his hands into his pockets. "Perhaps tomorrow?"

Clara took a deep, warm breath. "Yes," she said, her lungs feeling fuller than they had for a very long while. "I think I just might."

"You could come to the boiler house, after the Gilberts are asleep," said Will, giving her a shy smile. "It would be nice to have someone to talk to."

A tiny thrill shivered across Clara's shoulders. She must take extra care not to get caught by the Gilberts. If her aunt found out about her night-time visits to the gardens, she was sure to feel the wrath of her temper, and that was something to be avoided at all costs.

CHAPTER 10

Stolen Fruit

Clara rubbed the tiredness from her eyes as she sat at the breakfast table the next morning. She had only been staying with the Gilberts for six days, but so much had happened the previous day (and night) it felt like for ever. Mrs Gilbert had left a pot of porridge warming on the small stove before heading to the Big House for another day of housekeeping.

Mr Gilbert took a glass jar of honey from the shelf. The honeycomb glistened, jewel-like, in the shaft of sun hitting the table. The golden sweetness dripped from the wooden spoon into his milky porridge.

"Read there was another Zeppelin attack on the Norfolk coast," he said gruffly, glancing at his open newspaper.

His voice startled the tiredness from Clara's eyes.

"Two killed and some badly injured. This war is getting too close for comfort." He gave her a sidelong glance.

Clara's porridge stuck in her throat. She coughed, took a sip of her warm milk. Before they had stopped getting a regular newspaper at home, Clara had used to scour it for images of Zeppelins, those huge pencil-shaped floating machines with the capacity to drop bombs from their gondolas and blow entire houses to smithereens. The thought made her skin shudder and prickle in equal parts. Were the Germans really going to send hundreds of those flying machines to obliterate England?

The previous year, her cousins, who lived in the London borough of Shoreditch, had witnessed the bombing of the Empire Music Hall while a performance was taking place. The whole family had been so frightened that they had left their terraced house and moved to Cornwall. Wasn't Norfolk mostly open fields, like Cornwall and Devon? Maybe the Zeppelins would be heading for the south coast too – where her cousins were living and where Mother and Father were staying. An image of her father's cone of chips splattered on the seafront sprang into her head. Sickness washed over her. She placed her cup down and wiped her mouth with the back of her hand.

Mr Gilbert's forehead bunched under his dishevelled hair. He gave her a tentative smile and leaned forwards, placing his hands flat on the table. "Now look, Clara. The thing is—" He was interrupted by a firm rap at the door. It squeaked open, and cool air hurtled down the hallway.

"Mr Gilbert? Are you in?" asked a voice which Clara recognized.

Mr Gilbert tore his eyes away from Clara, sighed and pushed his chair back.

Clara stared out of the kitchen window. It was smeared and grimy with dirt. On the draining board were cloths and a bucket – presumably for Clara to start cleaning with. Clara thought about the cobwebs Mr Gilbert's hair had picked up when she had first arrived; the bumped skirting boards, the peeling wallpaper and crumbling plaster. Mrs Gilbert was a housekeeper, yet from her own house you would never guess that was her profession.

"Pineapples," Clara heard Robert say in the hall. Clara's thoughts stilled.

"How many?" Mr Gilbert said. His voice was high, tinged with panic.

"Three of them," Robert said. "Some peaches have been stolen too."

Clara thought about the fruits she had knocked from the tree the night before. The lime leaves Will had pressed between the pages of his notebook. The mandarin she had found on the tree stump and the one Will had seen in the reeds near the lake.

There was a lengthy pause.

Clara quietly pushed her chair back and crept to the kitchen door, placing her ear to the wood.

"Does anyone else know about this?" Mr Gilbert asked swiftly.

"No."

"Good. Keep it that way. If it is someone from the estate doing the thieving, we don't want them to know we are on to them."

"It wouldn't be anyone from here," Robert said.

Clara peeped around the edge of the door. Robert's face was flushed.

"Maybe. Maybe not," said Mr Gilbert, rubbing his chin.

"What about the Rifles Regiment?" Robert said.

"Them and all sorts are wandering the estate day and night. Shall I go and visit them?"

"No," said Mr Gilbert firmly – a little too firmly, Clara thought. "Keep your ears and eyes open though, lad. If you see anything suspicious, let me know."

"Yes, Mr Gilbert," Robert said, pushing his shoulders back. "You can trust me, Sir." Robert's Adam's apple bobbed in his throat, like a frog trying to leap from a lily pad.

"I know I can." Mr Gilbert paused, pushing his hands into his trouser pockets. "I also know you feel badly that you can't enlist next year when you're eighteen."

The colour in Robert's cheeks deepened. "I do, Sir. I feel very badly indeed. Seeing all those lads go off to fight. It makes me feel…a little useless."

"I know it," Mr Gilbert said softly. "But you need to concentrate on the gardens. They need you, as do I. There is much to be done." Mr Gilbert cleared his throat. "Right, come on. I want to see the results of this thieving for myself. I'll fetch my jacket." He walked back down the hall towards the kitchen.

Clara spun around and picked up the bucket and rags.

Mr Gilbert brushed past Clara as if she was invisible, spooned a final mouthful of porridge into his mouth, picked up his jacket from the back of his chair and left. "When the Earl finds out about this, there'll be hell to pay," she heard him mutter as he stomped down the hall.

Every window in the house rattled in agreement as the door to the gardens banged shut behind him. Clara stared after him, then placed the bucket and rags down and brushed off her apron.

Fruit had been lost as well as found. Could the stolen pineapples and the found mandarins be connected? She made a decision. As soon as she'd finished cleaning windows, she was going to explore the gardens and see what else she could find out before she visited Will that night. Will seemed to have a keen affection for the plants grown in the hothouses and was likely to be interested (and also upset) to hear about the stolen fruit.

CHAPTER 11

Tiger the Dog

The morning sun bounced from the windows of the hothouses, making Clara squint. The day was as crisp and golden as the apples on the trees. She chewed on a fingernail as she walked past the houses and down a slope to the Earl's summer house. It was partially built into the garden's inner walls, which sectioned off the different planting areas, its three huge windows facing the lake. The brick walls continued either side of the summer house, then turned at right angles towards the lake, enclosing a large lawn where Clara could imagine grand summer picnics and moonlit parties taking place. As she stood on the edge of the lawn near the water, she saw a sparkling chandelier hanging from the corniced

ceiling of the summer house. Perfect mandarin trees, oranges hanging from them like Christmas baubles, lined the back wall. White wicker chairs were scattered with silky cloudlike cushions. Sunlight reflected off the condensation on the inside of the glass.

A man was sitting on one of the chairs. His head was dipped towards a newspaper spread across his lap. A pipe was resting on the table next to him, small puffs of smoke reaching for the ceiling. There was no sign of the small girls with their nanny or the lady with the parasol who had chivvied them towards the summer house when Clara saw them yesterday. Perhaps the girls were having lessons with a governess in the Big House, learning about exciting things. Clara thought of Elsa and her other friends at school, and a pinch of sadness tightened her throat.

She bowed her head and secured the ribbons on her straw boater, remembering Mrs Gilbert's instructions about not making eye contact with the Earl. If she was to be staying with Mr and Mrs Gilbert a while longer, then she needed a friend. And she was hopeful she may have found one in Will. And if he was a friend, then maybe he would help her piece together the mystery of the fruit thief.

She remembered him saying that the boiler room was behind the summer house, underground, so she turned back towards the kitchen gardens, heading along the wall on the other side of the summer house lawn until she thought she might be in the right place. Her eyes skirted over a lone wasp dipping and dancing over two barrows of peelings to a low red-brick wall. The gardens here were in sharp contrast to the neatly manicured lawns in front of the summer house. Bales of straw were bursting from the strings tied around their middles and an assortment of rusting gardening tools were scattered across the rough ground. This must be a part of the gardens that the Earl and his family never visited.

Clara walked to the wall and ran her fingers over the bricks. It was then that she saw the steps, hidden from view behind two straw bales. At the foot of the steps was a blue wooden door, the paint cracked and peeling. She stood and gazed down at it. Will had to be in there. Was he sleeping? Maybe drawing in his notebook? Did he know anything about the stolen fruit? Maybe he had heard something while he was roaming the gardens at night? A horrible thought wormed its way into her gut…but before she had time to properly acknowledge it, she heard a voice.

"Alright, Miss?"

Clara swivelled around. A man and his small brown-and-white spaniel were standing there looking at her. The dog's head was tilted as if it wanted to ask Clara a question too, its pink tongue lolling. The man was chewing noisily on an apple, which was almost down to the core. He spat a pip onto the grass. The dog sniffed at it. "I'm George. One of the gamekeepers," the man said. "I've seen you about. I'm guessing you're Alfred's niece?"

Clara nodded, her fingers fizzing. Was George wondering what she was doing there? Did he know about Will?

"I'm just back from the woods. It's the start of the pheasant season," George said. "Although I reckon all that rifle fire in the nights is scaring them off. Didn't catch a thing this morning."

"Oh," replied Clara, staring at the gun he was carrying over his left shoulder. "You shoot…just birds?"

"Birds and deer – sometimes rabbits too. The Earl does like a slice of Cook's rabbit-and-rosemary pie. But we can't be choosy now, what with the war and so many men gone. Only ten men working on the estate now – used to be six times that." George sighed heavily, reached down and tickled between his spaniel's ears.

All those people to look after one Earl and his family, Clara thought. What would it be like to have people hunting, gardening, cooking and cleaning for you each and every day?

George looked over Clara's shoulder down the steps. "You were looking at the boiler house?" His dog scampered down the steps and began scrabbling at the door. *Click-click-click* went the dog's nails against the wood. It whined and *click-clicked* some more. George frowned. "Tiger, come back here," he said, giving the dog a whistle. But Tiger (who definitely did not live up to his name in looks) continued to ignore him.

"Tiger," called Clara. "Come on, boy." Maybe it could smell Will or hear him coughing? If George followed Tiger and started to investigate…

"It's a girl dog," George said tartly.

Boy, girl, did it matter? That dog needed to leave the door alone.

Clara ran down the steps and scooped Tiger up into her arms. The dog protested and wriggled like a furry eel.

"Careful, she bites," called George.

Clara held Tiger at arm's length, while the dog's jaws

gnashed and nipped at Clara without success. "If only it had been you in my nightmare, maybe I wouldn't have been so scared, and Mrs Gilbert would not have lost her hair," Clara murmured. The dog quietened and regarded her steadily. Then it yawned, its body going limp. Clara held the dog closer to her chest; it turned its head and licked her hand. Its tongue was rough and wet and made Clara giggle.

"She likes you," George said, tilting his head. At the top of the steps he took the dog from Clara and fondled its ears. "Nothing but trouble, this one," he said softly. "Quite useless as a hunter, but can't bear to get rid of the wee thing." His eyes flicked to the steps again. "What are you doing down this part of the gardens, anyway?"

Clara's brain whirred. She walked to one of the barrows of peelings, swatted away two more wasps which had come to join their friend, and lifted the handles. "I was about to take this to the compost," she said. The muscles in her arms groaned as she lifted the handles. She pushed it forward and it wobbled to the side, spilling peelings onto the grass. The metal handles dug into her fingers, which were already red-raw and cracked from washing windows all morning.

"What's going on?" Robert had appeared and set down the bale of straw he had been carrying on his shoulders.

"She's taking it to the compost," George said, throwing his apple core into the barrow.

Clara grunted as she tried to steer the barrow along the grass path towards the east wall where she'd seen the compost heaps on her wanderings, Tiger dancing and yapping around her feet.

"Clara?" Mr Gilbert came striding towards her, his face rosy.

"She's taking it to the compost," said George and Robert at the exact same time.

Clara could feel her cheeks flushing. She dropped the barrow with a *whump* and wiped her hands on her apron. "I'm just trying to be…useful," she said.

"Here, let me," Robert said, taking the handles from her.

"No, I can do it," Clara said. The barrow shook and swayed along the grass as Clara gritted her teeth, the three men following behind, picking up fallen peelings and throwing them back in the barrow as she heaved and pushed.

At last the compost heap was in sight. Robert

stepped forward to help Clara tip the barrow. "No, let me," Clara said breathlessly. The barrow tipped, the contents splurging onto the pile of decaying, sweet-smelling mulch.

From the corner of her eye she saw Mr Gilbert's lips were quirked into the smallest of smiles. "You'll find a wicker basket beyond the orchard against the back wall. Only pick the ripest of apples. A gentle tug and they should come loose. Tell Robert when you are done, he can load them onto the cart for the hospital." Giving Clara a quick nod, he strode back down the hill.

Robert grinned. "Looks like you'll be helping in the gardens then," he said. "I'm glad. You're a hard worker. I think we will get along well enough."

Clara grinned, bent down and stroked Tiger, who was still sniffing around her feet. George tipped his cap, whistled his dog and walked on.

Clara's shoulders ached. Her head was hot under her hat. Her thumb had a blister from clenching the handles of the barrow. Still, it felt good to be outside with everyone else – actually doing something to help the war effort.

But then that horrible wormlike thought that had been burrowing into her since she'd stood outside the boiler house returned. Will had asked Clara to keep his presence a secret. And what if there was more than one reason he was so keen to stay hidden? Could he have something to do with the missing fruit?

CHAPTER 12

Keyhole

That evening Clara curled up on her bed, thinking about Will. She had stumbled across him in a hothouse. He kept leaves from exotic plants in his notebook. He was alone in the gardens at night, which gave him the perfect opportunity to steal some of the fruit. But then again, he had seemed as upset as she was at the limes knocked off the little tree. And why on earth would he want to steal anything, especially if that might give him away? Her mouth was paper-dry from all the thinking. She drained the last of the water in her tin mug and glanced at the watch Father had given her for her last birthday. 10 p.m. Her aunt and uncle were early risers and so were normally in bed by now. Clara crept downstairs, pausing on the landing to listen for their snores.

Mr Gilbert's nasal warble curled under the door. Mrs Gilbert's didn't. A blade of light was spilling out from under the next door along, that of the locked woodland room. Clara silently placed the mug down, kneeled in front of the keyhole and peeped inside. Mrs Gilbert was sitting at the bureau in her white nightdress, her hair twisted over one shoulder, her hand busy writing. She stopped, tipped her face to the ceiling and massaged the back of her neck. Her fingers pulled and stretched the skin, as if she was kneading a lump of dough. "What am I to do? This can't go on," she murmured.

Clara pressed herself closer to the keyhole, the metal hard and cool against her face.

Mrs Gilbert folded the piece of paper and slipped it into an envelope. It was a letter. Was she writing back to Clara's mother? Could the heap of other envelopes on the bureau be six days' worth of letters *from* her mother?

An itchy scratch tickled the back of Clara's throat. An odd feeling was building behind her nose, like bubbles. The feeling grew bigger and bigger until Clara knew there was nothing she could do to stop it. Her knees dropped to the floor with a bump. She pinched her nose hard. Her sneeze was a cross between a hiccup and the sort of noise she imagined a hippopotamus might make if its nose was tickled.

The scrape of a chair being pushed back. Bare feet padding over wood.

Clara stood up in a rush and banged her elbow on the doorknob, which gave an insistent judder. *Oh dear*, she thought, rubbing her funny bone.

The door swung open. Mrs Gilbert's eyes were narrowed. She stared at Clara, at the mug on the floor. "Whatever are you doing?"

Clara picked up her mug. "I was thirsty," she whispered, glancing at the bedroom door, behind which Mr Gilbert's snores were still rising and falling. Thankfully the noise hadn't woken him.

"The kitchen is downstairs," said Mrs Gilbert.

"I was…just on my way there," said Clara quietly, holding the mug to her chest. She dipped her head and began to walk down the landing.

"Clara?"

Clara paused, turned. Mrs Gilbert was twisting the simple gold chain she wore around her neck. She had a sudden flash of memory of her aunt showing her the necklace when she last came to visit. She and Clara had been sitting on a patch of sun-bleached grass in the small back garden. "Alfred gave this to me for my birthday," Mrs Gilbert had said with a shy smile, when Clara had commented on how pretty the necklace was. "The day I went to work for the Earl and met my Alfred was the luckiest day of my life. I have truly never been so happy."

Clara stared at Mrs Gilbert for a second, trying to reconcile her dim but fond memories of her aunt with the formidable woman standing in front of her now.

"There are some things…you do not need to concern yourself with." Mrs Gilbert's voice wasn't cross exactly, more exasperated, like she had a problem which needed an answer.

"Goodnight, then," Clara said, wishing she had the courage to question Mrs Gilbert further, but knowing that if she did it would bring an ill-tempered glint to her aunt's eyes.

"Goodnight," Mrs Gilbert replied.

Clara smoothed her hand over the wooden banister and began to walk downstairs. She heard Mrs Gilbert lock the door of the woodland room and return to her own bedroom.

By now, Clara knew full well that when an adult said there was nothing to be concerned about, the mere act of saying those words often meant that there was. Clara's mother had insisted she should not worry about her father when he went to war and look how that had ended up. He left in 1915 shortly after Clara's eleventh birthday, just as the spring lambs had begun to dance in the fields. In early 1916 he had returned home, as a blizzarding storm bit at their cheeks. Clara had barely recognized him; his cheeks sallow, his lungs crackling and bubbling, a look of utter despair in his eyes. She pushed that particular thought away and clenched her jaw. If Mrs Gilbert was writing and receiving letters from her mother, she had an absolute right to know what they said. And clearly there was only one way to do that – she had to get inside the locked room.

CHAPTER 13

Notebook

Clara rapped her knuckles on the blue door of the boiler house as loudly as she dared. The night sky was peppered with clouds and stars, the wind curling her hair around her cheeks.

A smothered cough came from inside. "Clara?"

"Yes, it's me," Clara whispered.

There was the scrape of a key turning in a lock, followed by the creak of the door opening. Will stood in the shadows. "Come on, quickly," he whispered.

Clara stepped into the darkness and Will shut and locked the door behind her. As her eyes adjusted, she saw light at the end of a short corridor. There was the sharp strike and fizz of a match and then she was

blinking in the glow of an oil lamp swinging in Will's hand. The walls were rough and blackened, the air even warmer here than inside the hothouses. The sound of the nightly rifle fire was muffled underground – the opposite of in her attic room, where it bounced off the walls and felt like it was being absorbed into every surface (including her own self).

"This way," said Will. His feet were light on the brick floor, barely making a sound. Five steps down the corridor, they passed through another door which, again, Will shut behind them. Clara glanced at him as he turned the key. Her stomach was twisted into a knot, her mouth as dry as sand. *Mountain climbers. Hot-air balloonists. Surgeons. Be brave, Clara.* She slipped her hand into her pocket and gave the mandarin a squeeze. The size and weight of the fruit was comforting and yet also a reminder of her concerns. What if Will *did* have something to do with the fruit going missing from the hothouses? She was locked in an underground room in the middle of the night and nobody knew where she was. She was trying her best to be brave, but at that moment it seemed there was a high chance she had been spectacularly foolish in agreeing to come here.

The ceiling was almost low enough to touch. Pipes

– thick ones and thin ones – criss-crossed it like roads. Every few seconds they let out a soft hiss and vibrated, almost as if they were singing to one another. A gentle rumble and an occasional thump came from the black furnace squatting against the far wall, like a monster stirring in its sleep. Every surface was coated in a thin layer of coal dust – the small wooden table and chair in one corner, the heap of blankets on the floor. Clara could feel the dust settling onto her clothes and hair and skin. She remembered Will shaking out the blankets before he lay down to sleep under the blue moon. Now she knew why.

Will coughed again; a great, rasping cough which brought tears to his eyes. He pulled out a handkerchief and wiped them, then pulled on a thick glove and opened the door to the furnace. Red-hot embers glowed inside. He picked up a spade and shovelled in coal. The fiery embers spat in response. "I'm glad you came, Clara," he called over his shoulder. "Being down here day and night stoking this boiler can be…lonely."

"I suppose it must be," said Clara, a lurch of sympathy tightening her throat. "Are you paid for your work?"

Will shook his head. "My friend is doing me favour

enough by letting me stay here. I don't need money, just food and a place to sleep."

Then something caught Clara's eye on top of the pile of blankets. Will's notebook was open, the pages wafting in the warm air. Next to the book lay some leaves. She recognized the lime leaves, but there were other ones too – exotic and unfamiliar. Some were deep green and as large as a person's hand, some were smaller with serrated edges. They could only have come from the hothouses. She reached into her pocket and pulled out the mandarin. With a trembling hand, she lay it next to Will's notebook and the pile of leaves.

Will's shadow fell across her. "Oh. Why did you bring that?" he asked, staring at the fruit.

Clara planted her feet firmly on the brick floor, but her insides felt like the raspberry trifle her mother would make on a Sunday afternoon for tea. If she told Will that she suspected him of taking the fruit, she could say goodbye to the bud of friendship she felt blooming between them. She chewed on her bottom lip.

"What is it, Clara?" Will asked, taking a step towards her.

Clara looked at her boots. If she didn't ask him

about the thieving, the unsaid thought would hang between them like a festering weed. She dragged in a deep breath of dusty air and looked up. "Fruit is going missing from the hothouses. Pineapples, and other things too."

Will's eyes widened. "Missing?"

"Yes, stolen," said Clara. She swallowed. "Was it you?"

A laugh burst from Will's lips. "Me? You think I would steal the Earl's fruit?"

"Well?" Clara said. *Be brave. Be brave.* If she said it often enough, pretended hard enough, maybe it would become true.

"Look," Will said, picking up his notebook and thrusting it at her.

"At what?"

"This," said Will, pointing at a page.

Clara tentatively took the book from him. His finger was jabbing at a perfect pencil drawing of a mandarin attached to a willowy branch, its waxy leaves shaded so precisely they seemed to leap off the paper.

"It's lovely but—"

"Turn the page," Will said in a firm voice.

Clara looked at him. His eyes were fiery and bright.

She flipped the page with her forefinger to an exquisitely drawn map of the kitchen gardens, showing the winding brick wall, the planting beds laid out with miniature cabbages and leeks and carrots, the cottage Clara was living in – even the window of her room (which was open). If she squinted she could even see the candleholder on her window sill, a miniature drip of wax stealing down its side.

She turned to the next page, to a drawing of a hothouse. Below it was a cross section of miniature pineapples standing in rows. They were all different in shape – some conelike, some like pyramids – and each one was labelled.

"Black Antigua. This one is juicy and flavoursome – or so I hear. This Green Java is supposed to melt in the mouth. The Scarlet Brazilian – what a name, Clara! These fruits are magnificent, but I would never steal what's not mine to take. I hope to work in these gardens one day," Will said, waving his arms around. "I will have my own room with a view of the hothouses. I will look after the pineapples, see these queens of fruits grow from tiny plants."

Will's enthusiasm tugged a smile to Clara's lips. He didn't speak like someone intent on stealing the Earl's fruit. "How do you know so much about pineapples?" she asked.

Will's face dropped. He rubbed his nose and sniffed. "My mother and father. They had a smallholding – half a field where they grew fruit and vegetables to sell at the local market. But they were interested in fruit from faraway places too. Father wanted to take us to these places, show us how the fruits grew, maybe settle there one day. But then the war started."

"Oh." Clara closed the notebook and handed it back to Will. The boiler ticked and grumbled; the oil lamp flickered on the table, casting wobbling shadows around the room. "I'm sorry," Clara said. "I didn't mean to accuse you…"

Will shook his head. "I understand why you did. What with me hiding down here." He picked up the mandarin, cupping it in his palm. "You should eat this, before it goes bad."

Clara stared at Will and the mandarin. She had intended to eat it. But after hearing about the stolen fruit, something had held her back. "Do you think the thief could have dropped it by accident?" she asked quietly.

"On a tree stump?" said Will, his nose crinkling.

"And the one I found by the lake? It would have been a bit careless."

Clara shrugged. "It's just…an odd puzzle. To find fruit, but also to know that it's being taken."

"How did you find out fruit is going missing?" Will asked, frowning.

"I overheard Robert talking to Mr Gilbert."

Will's eyes dropped to the floor. He passed Clara the mandarin.

"Whatever is the matter?" asked Clara.

"Nothing," said Will.

Clara stared at him as he wiped a bead of sweat from his forehead using his jacket sleeve. "Really?"

Will pressed his hands to his ears. What had caused him to change? One minute he was discussing the mystery with her and the next…

The boiler hissed and ticked and waited with Clara for Will to speak. They waited for a few minutes. But that did not matter. Clara's father was always very patient with her when she did not know what to say, or rather knew what to say but did not know how to say it.

Will eventually opened his mouth, but no words came out.

"You can tell me, Will. I told you before, I am good

at keeping secrets." Clara pressed a hand into her pocket and felt the tip of her envelope.

Will took a deep breath. "He made me swear not to tell."

"Who did?" asked Clara.

Will walked to the pile of blankets in the corner, slumped down onto them and crossed his legs, resting his chin in his hands. "Robert. You see...he's my brother."

CHAPTER 14

Brothers

Clara blinked. Her eyes felt gritty from the coal dust, from discovering this new truth about Will. "But...you said a friend was helping you."

"I know," Will said quietly. "I lied."

Clara let the truth sink under her skin. She liked Robert, his talk of his hopes and dreams for the future, the fact he had helped persuade Mr Gilbert to let her work in the gardens. And he had kept a secret for her, by not telling Mrs Gilbert about her venturing into the hothouses. But Robert had a secret of his own – one which was locked up in the boiler house during the day.

"When Father died, we lost our cottage. It was tied

to the smallholding my parents ran. Robert said he would find me a job here. He's always looked out for me, made sure I had enough to eat and a roof over my head."

"But, this isn't *your* job, is it?" said Clara. "Robert told me it was the hall boy's job to stoke the boilers."

"Robert is slipping coins to Red, the hall boy," Will said. "If anyone asks, Red will say he is still stoking the furnace. He is helping us."

"But I have not seen this hall boy in the gardens even once," Clara said.

Will shrugged. "I imagine people are too busy to notice. The War is a big distraction."

"I suppose," said Clara.

"Robert said if anyone finds out about me, he could lose his job and then we would both be homeless. He said it's just for a short while, until he finds us somewhere to live."

Clara slumped down beside Will, glancing at a tin plate bearing a nibbled chunk of bread and a half-eaten apple, sitting on the little wooden table nearby. "He brings you enough to eat?"

Will nodded. "I don't go short. Sometimes I go foraging at night. I only take things which have fallen, or are growing wild though," he said, giving Clara an anxious glance.

Clara's jaw clenched. She had not given Will's circumstances much thought. It had been exciting to meet someone new, someone hiding in the gardens. But the reality of hearing about his hardships was making her regret eating that second slice of plum tart at tea. She should have saved it for Will. Next time she would.

Will coughed. It racked his chest and brought tears to his eyes again. Clara's own chest contracted. It reminded her of nights lying awake at home, listening to Father hacking away – the aching helplessness that there was nothing she could do to make him better. "Well, you can't stay down here. It's not good for your lungs," Clara said firmly.

"I sleep outside when I can," said Will, blowing his nose.

"But winter is on the way. What about when it rains, or when the gardens are thick with snow?"

Will shrugged, coughed again. "There are always the hothouses."

"But now that the fruit is being stolen, people will be keeping watch – Robert will be keeping watch," said Clara.

"I doubt that. Robert loves his sleep and his bed at The Bothy." Will fiddled with the cuffs on his jacket. "Please don't tell my brother that you know about me. He told me to keep hidden in the boiler house and not to speak with anyone. He'll be hopping mad if he finds out I've met you – especially as you're related to the head gardener and all."

"I promise I'll keep you a secret, Will," said Clara. "You can trust me."

Will flashed her a thankful smile.

An idea spun through Clara's mind. She grabbed at the threads of it. "So…if Robert isn't watching the hothouses, then you can sleep in the gardens. And if you are in the gardens…what if *you* watch for the thief?"

Will stared at her.

Clara sprang to her feet, clasping her hands together. "If you catch the thief, Mr Gilbert may be so pleased that he might give you proper work in the gardens. You might be able to live in The Bothy with your brother and get out of this dusty boiler house."

Will scrunched up his nose. His fingers were tapping on his knees, his eyes thoughtful.

A jolt of uncertainty wobbled Clara's legs. If Will got

caught, then he and Robert would both be in tremendous trouble. But then again, if he was successful, he might gain a permanent job and a proper bed to sleep in at night.

"Alright," Will said, in such a small voice that she wondered if she might have dreamed it. His face was lighter than it was before. "We'll try and catch this thief. We can't have them taking the Earl's pineapples."

"We?" Clara said, wide-eyed.

"Of course. It was your plan," said Will with a grin.

Clara felt a grin creasing her own cheeks. She reached into her pocket, pulled out the mandarin and handed it to Will. "Take it," she said. "I have plenty to eat."

"Thanks," Will said, placing it next to his notebook.

Clara let her mind roam beyond the boiler house and back towards the cottage, remembering all the little puzzles she had chanced on since coming to stay with the Gilberts: not just the missing fruit, but the found mandarins, the locked room in the cottage and its piles of letters on the bureau (which could well be from her mother). Thank goodness that Will was quickly becoming a friend and an ally. Perhaps he could help her solve the other mysteries of the gardens too.

Clara had one foot trapped in a swampy bog deep in a jungle. The harder she tried to yank her leg out, the deeper she sank into the vile-smelling mulch. *My boot will be ruined*, she thought. Mrs Gilbert would not be at all pleased. Voices sounded, muffled by the thick green foliage. "Help!" Clara called. "I am sinking." The swamp had risen up to her ankle; brown muddy water was seeping into her stocking. Clara's bottom lip trembled. She remembered what Father had told her, about pretending to be brave. "Hello, jungle. Hello, green leaves. Hello...swamp," she said in a wobbly voice. "Hello...hello...help!"

Clara woke with a jump, her heart jittering in her chest. She sat up in bed. Early morning light was spilling around the edges of the curtains, which were being sucked in and out of the open window in the breeze. Like her father, no matter how cool the weather she preferred to always sleep with her window open. That particular morning, the breeze came from the east. It was in a helpful mood and carried voices across the gardens and straight into Clara's bedroom.

"Don't meddle, Lizzy. Please leave things be," said Mr Gilbert.

The curtains whooshed backwards and forwards. Clara watched a spider repairing the edges of its web above her head, while trying to steady her breathing.

"I need to try, Alfred. It wouldn't be right to let things carry on as they are." Mrs Gilbert's voice was gentle, more how Clara remembered it from her visit years before.

"It's done. Nothing will change it," Mr Gilbert said in a voice that seemed as heavy as a sack of potatoes.

The breeze sang in Clara's ears – or was it a lengthy sigh coming from Mrs Gilbert's lips? She slipped out of bed and peeped around the edge of the curtain, shivering in the chill of the early morning. Her aunt and uncle were standing by the nearest hothouse – the one where the peach trees and limes and lemons grew.

Mr Gilbert took a step forward, clasping his wife's hands in his. His eyes seemed to be pleading with her.

Clara stiffened and held her breath.

Mrs Gilbert pulled her hands away. "I am so sorry… I must try."

They stood looking at each other for a few seconds, then Mrs Gilbert turned on her heel and headed up the slope towards the Big House.

Mr Gilbert pushed his hands into his pockets, watching his wife as she walked away. Once she was out of sight, he headed back towards the cottage.

Clara let the wind lift the curtain from her fingers.

Mrs Gilbert was keeping secrets too, Clara was sure of it. And today was as a good a day as any to try and find out what they were.

CHAPTER 15

The Tapestry

The cottage was still and resting after the early-morning bustle of washing, eating breakfast and clearing up. Mr Gilbert had eaten little of his slice of still-warm bread blanketed with a thin layer of strawberry preserve before leaving for the gardens. His eyes had been far away and lost in thought. What had Mrs Gilbert meant when she had told him things couldn't carry on as they were? Could it be something to do with the letters from Clara's mother?

Clara hovered outside the locked room and glanced up and down the landing. No one was there, but what she was about to do felt stealthy and underhand. Then again, it would also be underhand of Mrs Gilbert if she was keeping Clara's mother's letters from her. She lay a hand on the doorknob, bent down and peered through the keyhole. Was it her imagination or had the stack of envelopes on the wooden bureau grown? Had more letters from her mother arrived? She had been at the Gilberts' cottage for seven long days. Her mother must have written to her more than once in that time.

Clara's skin prickled. She didn't want to think badly of Mrs Gilbert – they were related after all – but she was making it extremely hard for Clara to find things to like about her. "I'm sorry that I do not like her," Clara whispered to the ceiling, the walls, the floor. The gloomy woodland wallpaper did not reply.

"You haven't seen your aunt in a few years, but you will get on with her well enough," her father had said confidently before she left. "I just wish the Earl would let her and Alfred have a little more time off from their work, so they could visit us more often. She has a lovely sense of humour. When I was a boy she could make me laugh so hard, sometimes I wet my trousers."

"Really, Gerald," Clara's mother had exclaimed in mock-horror, while Clara had giggled.

Clara scrunched her eyes up now, trying to imagine Mrs Gilbert's sour lips flipping into a sunny smile.

She clearly did not have a very good imagination for such things, for the image would not arrive in her head. She rubbed her eyes. She was getting distracted. With the Gilberts out of the house until teatime, it was the perfect opportunity to search their bedroom for the key to the locked room.

Clara had already searched the rest of the cottage. Just like the crooked door which led into the gardens, many of the cottage's walls stood at slight angles, which, alongside the ill-matched chairs, cushions, rugs and tables, made Clara feel a little unbalanced, like a tree breaking free from its roots. It was all quite the opposite of her small angular terraced home with its straight walls and ordered furniture. She had looked through the unevenly arranged key hooks near the back door (one bronze key had looked quite hopeful, but when she had fed it into the lock it had jammed, and it had taken her an age to wiggle it out), the woodwormy drawers in the kitchen (filled with ancient silverware in need of a good polish), and even the dusty outhouse stacked with logs. Yet it was all to no avail. There was no key to be found.

Clara pushed open the door of the Gilberts' bedroom. A path of sunlight gleamed on the floorboards, beckoning her forward. Taking a deep breath, she stepped inside. Laying both hands on the gnarly wooden dresser, she wondered for the hundredth time where Mrs Gilbert had hidden the key. She clearly did not want it to be found, so it would be somewhere private, somewhere no one would think to look.

Clara wiggled open each dresser-drawer in turn, revealing Mr Gilbert's faded cotton nightshirts and socks, followed by Mrs Gilbert's sensible (and rather big) underwear. She picked up a brassiere and gingerly felt inside. A flush stole onto her cheeks. If her mother knew she was rifling through her aunt's personal items, her opinion of Clara would surely sink to the bottom of the ocean. Clara set her jaw firm. Mrs Gilbert did not behave like an aunt or speak like an aunt – she did not dispense warm goodnight hugs and tender glances – so Clara would not behave like a niece. Instead, she would be an explorer of sorts, uncovering the secrets she was certain the Gilberts were keeping from her.

She carefully folded the brassiere and placed it back where she had found it. There were no hidden keys to locked doors here. Clara pressed her disappointment into the floor with the soles of her boots. Where else should she look?

She kneeled down and peered under the bed. Balls of dust gathered around its sturdy wooden legs, but that was all. Clara sat back on her heels and studied each corner of the room. There was no other furniture. The locked room next door had more furniture than the Gilberts' bedroom. Clara turned her gaze to the walls. Twisted vines snaked up the wallpaper, interspersed with bunches of faded purple grapes. The effect was gloomy and oppressive, just like the landing, just like the room next door.

Clara sighed, stood up and walked to the south-facing window which overlooked the lake. Father said if you had a difficult problem to solve, taking in a different view could sometimes help. Slow ripples crossed the water, as if someone had dropped a large pebble from up high. Clouds bubbled across the blue autumn sky, while a pair of swans swam, their beaks dipping and scooping. The window framed the scene, reminding Clara of the paintings she had been taken to see in the town museum back home.

Paintings. Pictures. Clara swivelled around. There were two pictures hanging on the wall. One above the dresser – a country scene of men forking bales of hay while swallows swooped in the blue sky. She reached up and lifted the picture away from the wall, ran a finger around the dusty frame. Nothing.

The other picture was a small tapestry, not much bigger than an open book. It hung on the wall above the wooden headboard. To reach it she would have to climb on the bed. She glanced at the door. All was quiet. Slipping off her boots, she clambered onto the bed and over the patchwork quilt.

Holding on to the headboard, she pulled herself upright. Her feet wobbled on the mattress as she looked at the tapestry. It was a pineapple – a twist of burnt-orange, brown and yellow threads. An embroidered pink ribbon bound the fruit to a clutch of purple figs and some emerald green leaves. The work was detailed and pretty, but some of the threads were loose, messy, like it had been finished in a rush. Had Mrs Gilbert made this? Clara searched for her embroidered initials at the base of the tapestry, but there were none.

Carefully lifting the frame away from the wall, Clara felt around the edges, then examined the thick board back. There was nothing there, aside from the name of the picture-framing shop and the date it had been framed: *Summers & Sons Framemakers of Abbeygate Street, 1914.*

The bang of the front door shutting made the window rattle. Clara's right foot slipped on the quilt. The tapestry frame fell from her hand, but instead of falling back into place against the wall, it trembled and nosedived behind the headboard to the floor below. The sound of splintering glass made her breath catch in her throat.

The clump of footsteps approached up the stairs.

Her surroundings imploded around her with a whoosh. How stupid she had been. She was not an explorer, a seeker of secrets. She was a small girl rooting around in a place she should not be rooting around in.

The door squeaked open and Clara bit the inside of her cheek until the rich ironlike taste of blood tingled on her tongue.

CHAPTER 16

The Key

Silence, aside from laboured breathing. Did the breaths belong to her, or the person standing in the doorway?

"What in heaven's name?" cried Mr Gilbert. His eyes were as wide as saucers. "What has happened here, Clara?"

"I'm…sorry," said Clara, unable to keep the quaver from her voice. "I was…looking at the tapestry. It fell. It broke. I will pay for the damage."

Mr Gilbert took a hesitant step towards her, then another. "You had best get down from the bed," he said quietly.

Clara's cheeks were burning. She half-fell from the

bed to the floor. She smoothed the wrinkles from the quilt and straightened the pillows. Bending down to pull on her boots, she saw a shard of glass lying next to them.

Mr Gilbert followed her gaze. "Oh dear," he said, rubbing his chin. He glanced at the empty spot on the wall where the tapestry had been hanging. "Oh dear, oh dear, oh dear."

"I will take it to the framemakers to get it mended. My mother gave me some money…for emergencies," said Clara in a rush.

Mr Gilbert sighed and shook his head. The shake was full of disappointment and it made Clara squirm. He bent down, reached under the bed and pulled out the tapestry. It was still attached to the board. Relief bubbled through her that the threads themselves did not appear to be damaged. Mr Gilbert passed the tapestry to Clara to hold while he fetched a brush.

If mild-mannered Mr Gilbert had thought the damaged tapestry frame warranted four *oh dears*, what would Mrs Gilbert's reaction be? Clara turned to place the tapestry on the bed. As she did, something floated to the floor. It was a scrap of folded paper which had been lodged between the tapestry and the board.

Mr Gilbert's feet thumped up the stairs.

Picking the paper up, Clara unfolded it. There was a single handwritten word: *Maestro*. What on earth did that mean?

Mr Gilbert coughed in the hallway.

Clara quickly refolded the paper and slipped it back under the tapestry.

Mr Gilbert came in and started to pull the bed away from the wall. The feet of the bed scraped on the wooden floor and the headboard rattled. But there was another sound too, so tiny, so minute, that Clara wondered if her ears were broken. It was the chink of something small and metallic against wood. Clara glanced at Mr Gilbert, but he seemed not to have heard.

As Mr Gilbert swept up the glass, Clara leaned forward. Hooked to the back of the headboard on a thick piece of string dangled a small bronze key. Clara's pulse thudded in her ears. She mentally kicked herself for not checking down the back of the bed earlier. It would have saved a whole lot of bother.

"I will talk to Mrs Gilbert," Mr Gilbert said, once the glass was swept up. He threw a wistful glance at the tapestry. It was the same kind of nurturing look Clara had seen him give the apple and plum trees in the garden. He opened the bottom drawer of their dresser and laid it carefully inside. "I'll try and smooth things over."

"Thank you," said Clara, clasping her hands together.

"No need to thank me yet," Mr Gilbert replied gruffly. He gave Clara a sorrowful look which burned into her bones and made her feel very small indeed.

Clara sat cross-legged on her bed, watching her spidery friends resting in the corners of their webs. One particularly large spider had spun its home between two of the attic beams. The web wafted in the breeze from the open window, like wafer-thin washing on a clothes-line.

Mrs Gilbert had returned to the cottage ten minutes before. As Clara watched the web, she could hear the rise and fall of Mr Gilbert's voice as he talked to his wife in their bedroom below. But she couldn't hear Mrs Gilbert saying anything at all. Clara had braced herself for Mrs Gilbert's sensible brown shoes to thunder up the stairs as soon as Mr Gilbert told her about Clara trespassing in their bedroom (on their bed, no less!) and the broken tapestry frame. But it hadn't happened.

Perhaps the tapestry did not mean as much to Mrs Gilbert as Mr Gilbert had implied?

Meanwhile, Clara couldn't stop wondering what the hidden slip of paper meant. *Maestro*. Was that not the name for a conductor of music? There was no piano or other instrument in the cottage. And Mrs Gilbert did not even like the gramophone – she said the noise gave her a funny head. It was all very odd.

But at least Clara now knew how to get into the locked room. She stood up and walked to the open window to suck in a breath of cool air. The light was fading, faint stars studding the sky. The front door banged shut so hard it made Clara's open window shudder in surprise. Mrs Gilbert was striding purposefully towards the hothouses. Where was she going at this time in the evening? Her head was lowered, and she was carrying a small wicker basket, a cloth covering whatever was inside. Her hair had come loose from her hat, tendrils snaking down her back. Clara felt a pull of recognition in her chest. Aside from the glisten of grey, Mrs Gilbert's hair had a similar wave to her own (and her father's). Even though Clara was not allowed to address Mrs Gilbert as Aunt, it was a sign of their relationship which could not be ignored.

Mrs Gilbert paused in front of the pineapple hothouse and pressed a hand to the glass. Her lips were moving, but the wind was not obliging that evening and did not carry her voice up to Clara's bedroom. She turned and glanced back at the cottage, as if checking to see whether she was being watched.

Clara ducked out of sight. A few seconds later she looked again. Mrs Gilbert was nowhere to be seen. Clara blinked, then strained her neck, searching the gardens, but there was no sign of her. Had she gone inside the hothouse?

Clara leaned her elbows on the window sill and waited and watched. The sky was blacker; it was getting more difficult to see.

"Clara?" Mr Gilbert was calling her.

She ignored him, peering out into the darkness.

"Clara." The sound of feet trudging up the stairs.

Clara reached for the window catch, swung it nearly closed and sat on the edge of the bed. She picked at a loose thread on the sheets and waited.

Her door creaked open. "Did you not hear me calling?" Mr Gilbert asked. His hair was sticking up in tufty peaks, even more bird's-nest-like than usual.

"No…sorry," Clara lied.

"Can you come and help me with tea? Mrs Gilbert has…an errand to run." His arms hung limp at his sides. His eyes seemed worn out, ready to close at any second.

Clara followed Mr Gilbert downstairs. She saw him glance at the locked door next to his bedroom as they passed it, then flick his eyes away. His hands balled into fists at his sides.

Determination grew behind Clara's ribs. As soon as she could, she was going to take the hidden key from behind the Gilberts' bed and find out if the answers to any of the puzzles that troubled her could be found inside the locked room.

CHAPTER 17

Will's Plan

As Clara helped prepare tea – buttering bread, cutting thick slices of ham and washing juicy red tomatoes – she wished she could run outside and check the hothouses. For she was sure that was where Mrs Gilbert had been going. With a basket. But why? For a second Clara thought... The ham knife slipped, narrowly missing her thumb. Could her aunt be...was she the...? No. Mrs Gilbert would not steal from the Earl. Clara's father had always said how dedicated Mr and Mrs Gilbert were to their jobs on the estate. That was one of the reasons they hardly ever came to visit. For them to steal and risk losing their beloved jobs was too foolhardy to even imagine.

Clara sat at the kitchen table and began to eat a slice of bread and ham (with a large helping of pickled cucumbers on the side). She glanced at Mrs Gilbert's waiting plate. She had not yet returned from her errand. She had been gone for over an hour. Mr Gilbert was chewing his sandwich slowly, occasionally glancing at the door. Perhaps now would be a good time to see if he had any answers to the unsolved puzzles rolling around in her head?

"What is the bedroom for, the one next to yours?" Clara asked Mr Gilbert, wiping cucumber juice from the corner of her mouth.

Mr Gilbert's jaw paused mid-chew. He coughed, as if a crumb was caught in his throat. He placed his sandwich down and slowly brushed flour dust from his hands, his gaze steady and fixed on Clara.

The door to the gardens opened and shut again.

Clara anchored her feet to the floor. She waited for Mrs Gilbert to come in, preparing for her steely gaze, sharp words and a suitable punishment. But instead, she heard her aunt's feet treading slowly up the stairs. Clara glanced at Mr Gilbert, who had started to chew again. He massaged his throat as if he was having trouble swallowing. He had still not answered her question about the room and it seemed as if he wasn't about to.

"I spoke with Elizabeth about the tapestry. She knows it was an accident," he said. His voice was low and crackly.

Guilt and sorrow burned in Clara's chest. It *had* been an accident. Even though she did not like Mrs Gilbert one small bit, it was somehow important that her aunt knew that. She pushed back her chair and strode to the door.

"Clara," Mr Gilbert said, but Clara ignored him, bounding up the stairs two at time before Mr Gilbert had even reached the kitchen door.

She stood outside Mrs Gilbert's bedroom. Funny noises were coming from inside, like a small animal was trapped and needed rescuing. Clara pressed her palms to the wood. The door creaked.

The animal noise stopped.

Clara gave a tentative knock. "Aunt...I mean, Mrs Gilbert. May I speak with you?"

Silence.

"I just wanted you to know...that I am truly sorry for breaking the tapestry frame."

More silence.

Then feet padded across the floorboards inside the room. The door creaked open.

Mrs Gilbert looked as Clara had never seen her before. High spots of colour bloomed on her cheeks. Her eyes were bright. Behind her, on the floor near the bed, Clara could see the basket Mrs Gilbert had taken into the gardens. It was empty, a red checked cloth neatly folded in the bottom.

Mrs Gilbert blinked, as if she had just woken and was seeing Clara for the first time.

Clara stared at her in surprise. Where was the punishment? The shouting and the sternness? It was like a giant paper straw had sucked away all of Mrs Gilbert's malice and anger, leaving her a hollowed-out eggshell.

"Go to bed, Clara. It's been a long day," she said wearily. She pressed the door shut.

Clara stood there for a second, placing a hand on the door again. She felt something curious inside – a pang of regret for Mrs Gilbert's weary, heavy eyes, and the weight which stooped her shoulders.

Clara watched the gardens from her window, just as Will had asked her to when she had left him the night before. The only problem was that her eyes were leaden with tiredness, closing every few seconds and then jerking open again when a fresh burst of rifle fire ricocheted through the night. She glanced at the spiders, who seemed oblivious to the noise. She wished for a second that she could join them on their webs, and have nothing more to worry about than keeping a neatly spun home and catching a fly or two for tea. Will had been wrong. She was not getting used to the Regiment's nightly practices. If anything, as the nights went on she was finding them harder to bear, a constant reminder of the waiting envelope from the War Office, and how the words inside might throw her family's life off-kilter. She and Mother and Father – they were like wooden skittles waiting to be knocked over by a large ball, with no one to pick them up, brush them down and stand them straight again.

Clara's candle burned low as she waited. She picked at a blob of wax which had dripped onto the window sill. She clenched her toes in her boots. She needed to think about horrible things, she decided. They would keep her awake in between the bursts of gunfire. Then, just before she could dig down into her darkest thoughts, she saw a single pinprick of light by the boiler-house steps – her signal. Throwing off the nightgown she had pulled on over her clothes (although there'd really been no need, as it never seemed to occur to Mr or Mrs Gilbert to check on her after she had gone to bed), Clara tiptoed down the stairs. She paused on the first floor, listening to the rise and fall of Mr and Mrs Gilbert's rhythmic snores. Then she ran lightly down the final set of stairs and opened the door to the gardens. Pulling it closed behind her, she rushed through the dark, her feet remembering the path like notes on a piano.

"You came," whispered Will, who was sitting on the low brick wall in front of the steps, a folded blanket on his lap.

"Of course," whispered Clara. "Why wouldn't I?"

Will smiled. "I'm just…glad, is all." He held something out in his hand.

Clara blinked in surprise. Another mandarin.

"It was at the entrance to the hothouse," Will said.

"How odd," said Clara, taking it from him and giving it a sniff. The citrus smell tickled her nose.

"Very," said Will.

"Could it be…the thief?" asked Clara, handing it back.

"There's only one way to know for sure, and that's to

catch whoever is doing this." There was something in the tone of Will's voice that Clara couldn't read.

"So, do you have a plan?" whispered Clara. "Are we going to hide in a bush or in the orchard? We would have a good view of the hothouses from up the slope."

Will shook his head, pushing the mandarin into his pocket. "I think we should watch from inside the pineapple house."

"What?" said Clara, her voice rising above a whisper.

Will pressed a finger to his lips.

"But that's madness. Surely Robert will be watching the gardens, like Mr Gilbert told him to. We'll get caught – and he'll be angry that you were out."

Will rubbed at his neck as if it was sore. "I told you, Robert sleeps like the dead. There is no chance he will be in the gardens tonight. Come on. Let's go catch the fruit thief."

Clara folded her arms around her middle, trying to quell the tiny shivers rolling through her body. Her mother had told her to look on her stay with her aunt and uncle as a little adventure. But she very much doubted her mother had imagined that adventure would involve Clara roaming the gardens at night with a new friend, trying to catch a pineapple thief.

CHAPTER 18

Pineapples

The pineapple hothouse was different at night. The dark mellow warmth expanded in Clara's lungs, while the occasional quiet gurgle of a hot-water pipe tickled her ears, as the spiky pineapple crowns quietly watched over them.

Will's feet came to a sudden stop and Clara bumped into his back.

"Sorry," she said hastily.

Will seemed not to have heard. The blanket he was carrying dropped to the ground. His head was bent over a plant pot. "Look at this," he whispered dully, placing a hand on the rim of the pot.

Clara frowned. The spiky leaves were there, but the

pineapple had been cut from the stalk. The other pineapples nearby appeared to be staring, their crowns of leaves bristling in shock.

"This Scarlet Brazilian had only just ripened," he said. His voice was thick with emotion. Clara watched as Will stroked the lengths of the leaves and examined the stalk the pineapple had been cut from. He dropped his hands to his sides, balled them into fists. "Taking things that don't belong to you...it makes my blood boil."

An onion-sized lump formed in Clara's throat. She reached down and picked up the blanket. "We need to catch whoever did this." She laid the blanket on the gravel under the planting bench halfway down the hothouse. They sat close, knees pulled to their chins, their backs to the panes of glass. It reminded Clara of playing house when she was small – how Mother would give her sheets that smelled of lavender water to drape over the living-room furniture, so she could make dens and have tea parties with her dolls.

They sat in silence, the earthy air warm and still. A drip of condensation plopped onto the bench above them. The windows shook and blustered in the wind.

"Do you find the days long here?" Clara asked after a while.

Will glanced at her. "Long?"

"I suppose I mean…it feels different here, there isn't much to do. I miss home. And school."

"You miss school?" Will said, raising his eyebrows. "Can't say I do. I prefer to be outdoors drawing. I suppose I do miss some of my friends, like Jonny. Once he stole Mrs Brown's glasses and put them on in the lesson. Everyone laughed, and it took for ever for her to notice. Probably because she couldn't see."

Clara smiled. It was nice talking to Will about school – it made home seem not so far away. "Today was curious," she whispered, picking up a piece of gravel and rolling it around in her palm. She told Will about the broken tapestry, the key to the locked room hidden behind the bed. Mrs Gilbert meeting Mr Gilbert near the hothouses, the wicker basket covered with a cloth.

The water pipes ticked and hissed.

"Mrs Gilbert had a basket?" Will asked.

Clara nodded.

"And she was near the hothouses?"

Clara nodded again. A wave of dizziness washed over her. "What? You think she could be taking the fruit?"

Will leaned forward. "It's possible."

"No." Clara picked up another piece of gravel and

placed it next to the first in her palm. Like two people standing shoulder to shoulder. She brushed the gravel from her hands. "My aunt and uncle are devoted to their jobs. They would never steal."

"There are food shortages. A sugar tax. People will pay good money for sweet things," Will whispered.

Clara thought about this. The Gilberts' cottage was musty and dusty and they clearly did not have a lot of money, but there was always plenty of food on the table. Whatever Will thought, she did not for one second believe they were stealing from the Earl.

Reaching into his pocket, Will pulled out his notebook. "After you left last night, I checked the hothouses. Made a list of the fruit which has gone missing."

Clara gasped. "But what if you had been caught?"

Will gave Clara a grim smile. "I was careful."

Clara leaned over and looked at Will's notebook, which was balanced on his knees. In the dim light she saw that, next to the list of missing fruit, he had drawn pictures of perfectly shaded peaches and three pineapples, the crowns twisting around the fruits, protecting them like vines. Next to them he had written *Scarlet Brazilians*.

"Why does the Earl like pineapples?" Clara asked.

"Status," Will whispered. "Did you know some fruiterers take the crown of a home-grown pineapple and attach it to one that has come from another country?"

"But why?"

"To deceive the dinner guests – make them think it was grown in the hothouse of their host."

Clara gazed at the fruits. A small bead of affection for them was growing inside her – perhaps not as much affection as Will had for them, but affection all the same.

"Pineapples used to be grown in horse manure to keep them warm. Imagine the smell." Will held his nose and wiggled his eyebrows.

Clara stifled a giggle. Will was like his brother Robert in some ways – the freckles which bounced on their cheeks, the way their noses crinkled – and in other ways not at all. When Robert spoke about fruit and vegetables, he was interested in how many people they would feed. But to Will, the fruits were so much more than that.

A feeling was building inside her, like a stream welcoming meltwater from thawing mountains. The tightness in her shoulders which had been there since she had arrived at Gardener's Cottage was sliding away. She reached into her pocket and pulled out the envelope; placed it on her lap.

"What's that?" Will whispered.

Clara sucked in a lungful of warm air. "A letter," she said. "One that doesn't belong to me."

CHAPTER 19

War Office

The War Office logo had smudged from the many times Clara had pressed it while trying to imagine what the words in the letter might say. "My brother Christopher. He is at the Front in France. At least... I think he is."

Will drew in a sharp breath.

"I...took this from the post-boy. I wasn't going to keep it, but then I was sent away, and Father and Mother left and it was too late. I was going to give it to Mrs Gilbert when I arrived. But...we don't get on well and she would be very cross that I have kept it for so long." Tears burned the back of Clara's throat. She picked up the envelope and cradled it in her palms.

"We received a pink telegram when Father died. It's not one of those. It might not be bad news," said Will quietly.

"But it might," Clara said in a small voice. "And I don't think Father or Mother could bear that. Neither could I." With a sigh, she slid the envelope back into her pocket. "If something has happened to Christopher and Father finds out, it might stop him from getting better. But Mrs Gilbert said my mother has written and I am to stay here longer. That must mean Father is worsening anyway." Misery and confusion slumped Clara's shoulders forward.

Will shuffled a little closer to Clara. His arm nudged hers. "But they report war casualties and deaths in the newspapers. Surely your parents must already know if something has happened to your brother?"

Clara shook her head. "Mother became obsessed with reading the casualty lists when Father was in France. Her hands would shake as she read through the names of all the men injured and dead."

Clara rested her head against the side of the bench, remembering the evening earlier that year when the newspaper had dropped from her mother's hands to the rug like a sail. Mother had clapped a hand to her mouth as tears leaked from her eyes. Christopher had kneeled on the living-room rug, smoothed the paper across his lap, his wild eyes scanning the many names listed.

"Your father is injured…not dead," her mother had croaked. She and Clara and Christopher had formed a tight huddle on the floor, their arms twisted around one another in relief.

Clara blinked the memory away. "When Christopher left, Father made Mother promise they would not read the casualty lists in the newspapers any more as it was too upsetting. They said any news would come by telegram or letter. It has, but they just don't know that yet."

"You should open it," Will said. "Go on – open it now. You can't pretend you don't have it. Look at the stamp, Clara. The War Office. It should be opened straight away and then you should tell Mrs Gilbert. What if Christopher is lying in a hospital somewhere all alone?"

"But he would have doctors and nurses looking after him," Clara whispered helplessly, trying to block out thoughts of her brother bandaged from head to toe and calling out for his family, who were nowhere to be seen. She twisted her hands together in her lap, remembering the sting of Mrs Gilbert's hand against her cheek. She could not and would not give the letter to her aunt.

The windows rattled gently in the wind. A scuffle on the gravel outside.

"What was that?" whispered Will.

Another scuffle.

Clara's breath caught in her throat.

A scrabbling, sniffing noise just beyond the glass.

"An animal – a rat maybe," Will whispered. "On the hunt for some food." He brought his hands to his cheeks and twitched his fingers like whiskers.

Clara rolled her eyes, smiling. The weight of her secret felt a fraction lighter now that she had shared it. She focused on one of the pineapples sitting proudly in its planting bed, the thin crown of leaves, the quilted fruit. Will was right. She should open the envelope. She *would* open the envelope. But once she did, she knew that things would be different. And sitting there, in the warmth, listening to the *drip-drip-drip* of condensation, a new friend by her side, she wasn't so sure she wanted things to change quite yet.

Clara started awake. Will was nudging her in the side. A cold trail of drool was running down her chin. She wiped it away with the back of her hand and got up.

"It will be dawn soon," whispered Will, folding the blanket. "No one came to steal the fruit."

They crept out of the hothouse into early morning mist, which swirled over the gardens. There was a sudden sound of footsteps on the grass approaching them, boots sliding over the heavy dew.

"Quick," hissed Will, grabbing Clara's arm and pulling her back down the steps. They cowered by the door as the footsteps grew nearer.

Clara had the same feeling she used to get when playing hide-and-seek with Christopher. She would always cover her eyes in her hiding place, believing the act of doing so would make her more invisible. The feet were going to pass in front of the hothouse entrance. Clara squeezed her eyes shut.

Stomp, stomp, stomp.

Will nudged her in the side as the sound of the footsteps retreated.

Clara flicked her eyes open.

Will's eyes were wide, excited.

"Mrs Gilbert," he whispered. "Where's she going?"

Clara stood and crept up two steps until she could see into the gardens. Mrs Gilbert was receding into the mist like a ghost, a basket swinging from her right arm like an unlit lantern. A bustle of thoughts zipped through Clara's head. How peculiar. What was Mrs Gilbert doing up so early? And most importantly, what was inside that basket she was carrying?

CHAPTER 20

The Soldier

Will and Clara followed Mrs Gilbert into the woods at a distance, far enough away so they could not hear her footsteps and she could not hear theirs, but close enough that they could just see her through the mist. Sticky mud clung to Clara's boots. She breathed in the perfume of moss soaked from the previous night's rain, and damp rotting wood. They crept past gossamer spiderwebs hung with dew, trod over dusky copper-tinged leaves. Mrs Gilbert paused next to a bramble bush laden with ripe blackberries. She picked a handful of berries and ate them, tipping her face up to the near-bare boughs and the sky beyond.

Will glanced at Clara where they were hiding behind

the thick trunk of an oak tree, and raised his eyebrows. Clara raised hers in return. Mrs Gilbert seemed different, her tread even more purposeful than usual. Where was she going?

They followed quietly until Mrs Gilbert paused again near two trees which had been felled. Will and Clara stole closer, sneaking behind the thickest of the tree trunks, using the mist to hide themselves. Clara's heartbeat pulsed in her ears. If Mrs Gilbert walked back the way she had come, they were very likely to be discovered.

Mrs Gilbert placed her basket on the leaf-strewn woodland floor, next to a flush of fungi that were sharp white against the browns and greens.

A midge fussed around Clara's face. She swatted it away, then curled her fingernails into the bark of the tree trunk she was pressed against.

A noise then. The sound of snapping twigs, the rustle of leaves.

The light was turning a soft pink through the mist. A moustached man in a green uniform emerged – a soldier.

"Morning, Lizzy," he said in a low voice. "I appreciate you coming out of your way. We start training early today." He glanced at his watch as the mist ebbed and flowed around them. He cleared his throat. "There is talk we'll be going to the Front in a few days."

Mrs Gilbert's face fell. "Oh, Thomas."

The rough bark dug under Clara's fingernails as her grip on the tree tightened. Mrs Gilbert knew this soldier well enough to call him by his first name.

Thomas gave Mrs Gilbert a small, cracked smile. His eyes were brimming with regret. "Seems like it's not meant to be then." He picked up the basket, lifted the cloth and peered inside. "Thank you," he said. "I just wish I could do something to…" Thomas suddenly bent over, his shoulders beginning to shake. He placed the basket on the ground and brought his hands to his face. A throaty sob burst from his lips. Then another. And another.

Clara stared at Thomas, rashes of goosebumps springing up on her arms and the back of her neck. Soldiers did not cry. They were strong and brave. When her father had returned from the War, when Christopher had said goodbye to them all, his back straight and proud as he walked down the street, Clara had not seen even a smidgen of moisture in their eyes, just a grim resolve that they should make the best of a terrible situation.

Mrs Gilbert took a step forward and placed a tentative arm across Thomas's heaving shoulders.

"I'm sorry…I'm sorry…" he gulped.

"I am the sorriest," said Mrs Gilbert in a low voice. Her face was as pale as chalk through the swirling mist.

"It is not your fault. I do not blame you. You know that," Thomas said through hiccupping breaths.

The lack of sleep, the stealthy walk through the woods, the crying soldier – it was all a little dizzying. Clara suddenly feared she might keel over, like she was a tree being felled herself. She took a whisper-quiet, steadying breath and glanced at Will, who was transfixed by the scene before them.

Thomas straightened, pulled a handkerchief from his pocket, blew his nose noisily and roughly wiped his eyes and cheeks. The sounds echoed through the just-waking woods. A bird cawed in the trees high above their heads.

Mrs Gilbert glanced behind her, in the direction she had come. "I must be getting back," she said in a small voice.

Clara gave Will an anxious look. He gestured for her to move around the tree trunk to hide them better from the path. Clara crept forwards, feeling the warmth of Will's breath on the back of her neck as he followed close behind.

"Of course you must," Thomas replied.

"If I don't see you again, please take good care," Mrs Gilbert said. Picking up her skirts, she flashed Thomas a sad smile and walked away. Thomas watched her until she was out of sight.

Will's forehead was bunched into tiny lines as they watched Thomas turn and disappear into the thinning mist. The sound of his boots cracking twigs drifted back to them.

"Shall we?" Will whispered, looking after him.

Clara bit her bottom lip. Mrs Gilbert was heading back to the cottage. What if she went up to the attic to check on Clara and found her missing?

Be brave, Clara thought. She would just have to come up with an excuse for her absence, like an early-morning walk to watch the sun rise, or getting a head start on the apple-picking for the next hospital delivery. She nodded at Will and watched his face mirror how she felt inside – full of purpose, determined to crack this puzzle. She wondered if he was also feeling the deep seated unease which sat heavy as an iron bar in the pit of her stomach.

What had caused the soldier to be so upset? And what was in the basket?

Thomas kept a steady pace, and Clara's legs began to ache as they followed. Soon he had pushed ahead out of sight and they were tracking him by sound alone. Clara longed to sit for a while and catch her breath. She longed even more for her bed. But they had to find out where the soldier was going.

Suddenly she realized something was different. She paused. There was no thud of Thomas's footsteps or the rustle of boots on leaves as he pushed his way through brambles. A bolt of terror clambered up her spine.

"Oi…you there!" The voice startled a pheasant from the bushes. It whirled into the air, its wings beating against the leaves like a carpet brush. There was the crackle of branches. Was that the sound of a rifle safety lock?

Will turned and threw a desperate glance at Clara. "Run," he breathed.

Clara swung round; the sound of Thomas's heavy breaths rasped to her right.

Will grabbed Clara's hand as he belted past, dragging her through the undergrowth back the way they had come.

Footsteps were gaining on them behind. Clara could

still hear the soldier's panting dog-like breaths.

The mist was hiding them from Thomas. But it was also their enemy, causing them to swerve around tree trunks that appeared from nowhere, snag their clothes on branches, and trip over logs.

"In here," whispered Will breathlessly, dodging to the right. He pulled her down behind an upturned tree, its roots reaching into the air like witches' fingers.

Clara could see Will's pulse hammering in his temple. He jammed his hands over his mouth and stifled a cough which made his eyes water.

Thomas's feet were still thundering through the undergrowth towards them.

Hiding. She and Will were always hiding. From the thief. From Robert. Now from the soldier Mrs Gilbert was so friendly with.

The sound of Thomas's feet halted.

Clara threw Will an anxious glance. He motioned for her to lie down alongside the fallen tree. There was just enough room to crawl into the gap between the curve of the tree and the soil. She moved her body stealthily, mirroring Will as he slid into the narrow space. They lay head to toe, the soles of Will's muddy upturned boots almost scraping Clara's hair.

A stick was swiping through the undergrowth. It swished and beat through the brambles, searching them out. A blackthorn bush rippled. Clara twisted her head to the left and saw large army boots walk past the fallen tree.

She held her breath. Will was so motionless she wondered if he was still alive, until she saw his left foot twitch.

The swishing stick grew fainter, until they could hear it no more. They continued to lie in the mud, barely moving, hardly breathing. Will's boot eventually nudged Clara's forehead. "It's clear. Let's go."

Clara rolled out from under the tree. Her apron was streaked with mud, the dress sleeve she had snagged on a branch was ripped. Will's cheeks were imprinted with leaves, his hair standing in tufty spikes.

"That was jolly close," he said with a grimace, brushing the mud from his trousers. "What was that all about, do you think?"

"I don't know," said Clara. "But it was rather terrible seeing that soldier cry."

"It was," Will agreed. "What do you think was in the basket Mrs Gilbert gave him?" he asked, leaning against the fallen tree. He snapped a twig from a branch.

"I'm not sure. Why?"

He jabbed the tree with the stick, like it was a spear. "Mrs Gilbert – I think she is stealing the fruit. She's giving it to the soldier."

Clara's mouth felt full of cotton. "No, Will. It just doesn't seem…right. Mrs Gilbert wouldn't do that."

"So why is she creeping around, meeting him in the early morning when everyone else is asleep?" Will said.

Clara scuffed at the leaves with her boots. Could Will be right? She hated to think anything so awful of her father's sister, but Mrs Gilbert really hadn't been very nice to her at all since she arrived. Maybe Clara just had to accept that Mrs Gilbert was a truly bad egg.

"You need to get into that locked room in the cottage today. Maybe there are other things hidden in there, besides the letters your mother is writing to you," Will said urgently. "Things like the stolen fruit."

"Well, I don't know about that," whispered Clara doubtfully. Her thoughts were hazy and slow, as if she was swimming underwater. Why was Will so insistent that Mrs Gilbert was responsible for the thefts? His fingers tapped against his trouser legs as they walked back through the woods, his eyes flitting to the gaps between the trees, almost as if he was looking for someone. The encounter with Mrs Gilbert and the soldier had clearly unsettled him. Instead of finding answers by following Mrs Gilbert, Clara had more questions than ever before.

CHAPTER 21

Letters

Mr Gilbert was in the kitchen pouring a mug of tea when Clara returned. "Morning," he called down the hall. "Nice to see you up and about so early. Mrs Gilbert was out at dawn too. Did you see her?"

"No," Clara called back, stifling a yawn. She folded her arms to hide the worst of the muddy stains on her apron.

Mr Gilbert walked into the hall, cradling his mug. A fleeting frown crossed his face. "What happened to your dress, Clara?"

In her eagerness to conceal the apron, she had forgotten about her ripped sleeve. Clara felt a warm flush stealing onto her tired face. "Oh, I...caught it on a bramble. I will mend it myself."

151

"Lizzy will do it for you," Mr Gilbert said with a smile. "She's always had a talent for sewing, knitting and suchlike."

Clara remembered the tapestry lying forlornly in the Gilberts' dresser upstairs. Mrs Gilbert might have a talent, but Clara certainly wasn't going to give her any cause for further crossness because of a small thing like a ripped sleeve.

"You can help with the apple harvest this afternoon," Mr Gilbert said. "Robert will be taking a cartload to the Red Cross hospital in town tomorrow. You can accompany him if you like? Must be a little boring for you, stuck out here in the countryside."

Clara gave him a limp smile. If only he knew that, right now, she had never been less bored in her entire life.

"Right-ho. Best get to it. Those under-gardeners are probably still in their beds. Good mind to throw a bucket of water over the lazy whatsits." Mr Gilbert smiled. It crimped his weary eyes and made Clara smile properly in return. "You look as tired as I feel, lass," Mr Gilbert said, walking to the door. "I hope Robert isn't working you too hard."

"Oh, not at all. I like being busy," Clara said. "Less time to…think."

Mr Gilbert paused, his hand on the doorknob. He turned to face her. "Yes. I see that." He took a slurp of his tea, sighed heavily. "Things will right themselves soon enough." His look was kind. A sudden urge bustled through Clara – to throw her arms around him, feel the bristles on his chin on top of her head, smell the reassuring scent of soil, apples and vegetables. But then he was gone, closing the door quietly behind him, and Clara was left with an image of Father in her head as she trod wearily up the stairs towards her bed for a secret daytime sleep.

The early-morning mist had burned away, exposing a weak sun and lengthening shadows. It was late, well after lunch, and Clara was surprised to find she had slept all morning. She glanced in the mirror at the pillow crease on her right cheek and the plum-coloured bruises under her eyes.

Wasting no more time, she went to retrieve the hidden key from the Gilberts' bedroom. The metal felt cool against her hot palm. Back out on the landing, she quickly pushed it into the keyhole of the mysterious room and turned it with a click. Twisting the doorknob, she opened the door and stepped inside, her stockinged feet as soft and silent as Neptune the cat's. She locked the door from the inside, dropping the key into her apron pocket.

The temptation to rush to the bureau and the small pile of letters made Clara's fingers tingle, but there were things she needed to do first. "Hello, bed," she said. She ran her fingertips over the cream-painted metal bed frame. She picked up the crocheted blanket and stroked the burnt-yellow and forest-green wool. This blanket had been made with love and care. There were no dropped stiches and ragged edges like the one on her bed. She refolded it and walked to the bureau, then looked through the window beyond it. "Hello, window." The view was similar to the view from the Gilberts' room: the silvery lake, the ploughed fields, the trees beyond erupting in volcanic yellows, oranges and russet-reds.

"Hello, bureau," Clara said finally. The wood was cool and shiny, and smelled of polish. She wiggled open the largest of the drawers. Piles of envelopes sat in neat rows. There were too many here to all be from her mother. A jolt of cold wormed its way down Clara's spine. She wiped her damp palms on her apron and picked one up. It was not addressed to her or Mrs

Gilbert. It was not addressed to anyone at all. Clara frowned. She flicked through the other envelopes. They were all blank, and all sealed.

Clara shut the drawer and opened the one beneath. She held her breath, half-expecting Will's theory about Mrs Gilbert to be right – that she would discover a clutch of peaches and some pineapples. But there was no fruit, just more sealed envelopes.

Clara picked up the top envelope from the stack on the bureau. It, too, was blank. The ones beneath it collapsed like a fan. She turned the envelope over. This one had not been sealed. She put it down. Picked it up again. She thought about the letter from the War Office nestling in her own pocket. Guilt prickled across the backs of her arms, making the hairs stand on end. Slipping her fingers into the envelope, she pulled out a single sheet of folded paper and began to read.

October 1916

My Dearest,

Autumn has finally arrived on the estate. The trees are bursting with apples and pears and plums. There is so much fruit that the Earl has ordered we send some to the military hospital in town. The young *under-gardener, Robert, loads the crates into the cart and hitches up Kitty the horse. Remember how you love Kitty? You press your nose into her flank and breathe in her warmth. I thought I glimpsed you in the woods again this evening, heard your laugh. It was not you, but I sorely wish it had been. I long for us to picnic together in the hothouses, spread out the blanket and sit among the sweet-smelling fruits as you amuse me with your stories of home.*

Your fondest,

Lizzy

"It's just so odd. Who is Mrs Gilbert writing to? And where were the letters from my mother?" Clara whispered to Will in the pineapple house that night.

Will bent over one of the plants, stroking its leaves tenderly. "It's strange, alright."

Clara recognized the look on Will's face. It was the same as the one that had bunched his eyebrows together when he came up with the idea that Mrs Gilbert was stealing the fruit. "What is it?"

"She's writing letters to someone with no name… she's secretly meeting a soldier in the woods…"

Clara folded her arms. "We don't *know* they are meeting in secret."

Will rolled his eyes. "Really?"

A quiver of irritation stiffened Clara's jaw. Will had been quick to decide her aunt was up to no good. But were those letters intended for Thomas? Clara thought not. The tone of Mrs Gilbert's writing was tender, but in the way you might talk to a good friend. It was true that Mrs Gilbert had been quick to comfort the crying soldier, but there had been an awkwardness to their encounter that led Clara to firmly believe the letters were not meant for him. And besides, if she *was* writing to the soldier, why not simply give him the letters in person?

"We mustn't let your aunt get her hands on this Scarlet Brazilian," said Will firmly. His eyes glinted in the darkness. "Three years it's taken to grow this big. That's why these plants are so tremendous. They put so much time into ripening. It's not like an apple or a plum that takes a few months and then it's ready to be eaten."

Clara went to stand beside him. "But we've been watching for two nights now. Maybe the thief has given up."

"You mean maybe Mrs Gilbert has given up." Will's mouth was set in a hard line. "We'll just keep watching," he said, darting a glance at the door. "She's bound to take some more fruit soon."

Clara gave Will a doubtful look. She walked the length of the planting bench, examining each pineapple in turn. It was just so very hard to believe that her own aunt was responsible for taking the fruits. What would Father say? What would Mr Gilbert say if Will was right?

"I'd love to eat a home-grown pineapple one day," Will said, following Clara along the bench, "and see if it's as sweet as people say. We would sit in the Earl's summer house and have people wait on us with silver trays and fine china."

Clara smiled, the muscles in her jaw relaxing. "People would curtsey and bow in our company."

"And I would have clean nails and a fancy suit," Will whispered with a grin.

"Clean nails?" snorted Clara softly. "Chance would be a fine thing."

Will nudged her in the side with his elbow.

She did the same in return. Warmth spread through her. Contentment arrived in the strangest of guises – in a hothouse at night with a boy she barely knew, while trying to work out exactly what her aunt was up to.

Chapter 22

Delivery

Clara was shaken awake by Mrs Gilbert. Her eyes sprang open. Mrs Gilbert patted her hair (perhaps remembering the hair she had lost the last time she had been in Clara's room), then took a step backwards. Why had Mrs Gilbert woken her? For one horrible second she thought Mrs Gilbert had come to tell her she knew Clara had been into the locked room and read her secret letters. For another horrible second Clara wondered what her punishment would be. The door to her attic room had a keyhole. Did Mrs Gilbert have the key to hand, ready to lock Clara in? The thought squashed the breath from her lungs.

"In the nine days you have been here, I have never

known a girl sleep so much," Mrs Gilbert said with a sniff. She walked to the window, opened the curtains and tutted loudly. "You will catch a cold, Clara, leaving this window open all night. I have brought you another blanket." Mrs Gilbert's offering was folded on the end of the bed.

Clara sat up and pulled the blanket towards her as she readjusted her thoughts. "Thank you," she said.

Mrs Gilbert gave her a small nod as she banged the window shut. The spiders above Clara's head shuddered in their webs.

"Father says fresh air is good for the soul," Clara said, holding the blanket to her cheek.

"Does he now?" Mrs Gilbert gazed out of the windows to the gardens as she smoothed the curtains. "He could be right," she murmured. Her voice was gentle, more how Clara remembered it sounding. "Mr Gilbert told me you are helping Robert take the vegetables to the hospital today," she said, letting the curtains fall from her fingers.

Clara held her breath for a second or two. Was Mrs Gilbert going to say she could not go?

"Just...stay with Robert. Don't go wandering off on your own," her aunt said. "Robert's a good lad. He's got a lot of enthusiasm for sorting out vegetables for the hospital deliveries. I imagine it makes him feel useful, after his disappointment at not being able to enlist."

Clara's mouth began to tickle into a smile. She stopped it in the nick of time, pressing a hand to her cheek to remind herself of Mrs Gilbert's slap. Her aunt was like a hot-water bottle, switching from cold to hot and then back again. When her face and voice thawed, Clara could almost see the woman she remembered and the sister her father talked fondly about. The kind of girl who liked climbing trees and making dens and staying up late into the night chatting with her brother. What had happened to turn that girl into the woman who wrote secret letters and might possibly be stealing fruit from the Earl? Clara wished she could find out. And maybe, by solving the other mysteries that dwelled in these gardens, she would.

Mr Gilbert had seen Clara and Robert off in the horse and cart, and told Robert not to let Clara out of his sight.

"There's no need for Clara to come. I can take the vegetables to the hospital on my own," Robert had said, glancing at Clara, who was stroking the knots from Kitty's mane.

Mr Gilbert had shaken his head. "Two people will get the job done more quickly. I need you back here in the gardens as soon as possible, Robert."

"It's heavy work, lifting those crates," Robert had said, taking off his glasses and cleaning them on his shirtsleeve.

"Clara will manage," Mr Gilbert said, throwing a glance in her direction. "She's a strong lass."

Robert had shrugged, but he had not given Clara his usual cheery smile. Maybe he thought she was too weak, too small and girlish to help take the crates of vegetables and fruit into the hospital. Clara had pressed her lips together. She would just have to prove him wrong.

The cart jolted them from side to side as they headed down the long driveway and out of the estate. Clara glanced behind her at the tightly packed crates of vegetables covered with canvas sacks. Mr Gilbert had said it was the Earl's largest donation yet to the Red Cross auxiliary hospital in town. She shifted in her seat, slipping her hands into her apron pockets for warmth, but also to check that the three things she had brought with her were still there:

The envelope from the War Office (which, despite Will's encouragement, she was no closer to opening).

The tapestry, taken from the drawer in the Gilberts' dresser and carefully separated from its board. (Even if Mrs Gilbert was sour, Clara had a strong sense she needed to mend what she had broken, for Mr Gilbert's sake if nothing else.)

Her coin purse (which hopefully contained enough of her parents' emergency money to buy a new tapestry frame, and which was also hiding the small piece of paper she had found behind the tapestry that said *Maestro*).

The cartwheels jolted over the cattle grid and they passed through a pair of huge iron gates. On each gatepost balanced an elegant, carved stone pineapple. These fruits! Clara had lived a whole life not thinking about them, and now she could not escape them.

Robert was quiet as they drove down the country lanes, his feet jiggling on the wooden boards. He held the reins tight as Kitty clip-clopped her way down the hill and into the small market town. They trundled past red-brick cottages, and a forge where two women wearing blue headscarves were shoeing horses. Kitty trotted past more women, chatting and laughing while they tended to a field of hulking pink-and-black pigs. The smell from the field was pungent, and Clara held her nose.

Robert glanced at her and smiled.

Occasionally they were overtaken by stuttering motorcars driven by smartly dressed men in hats, women in elegant coats perched beside them. Why were these men not at war? What were they doing to help the war effort, for surely everyone must want to do their bit?

As the streets narrowed and they entered the town, they passed a church with stained-glass windows that winked in the sunlight. Robert slowed Kitty to make way for a military funeral. Clara could not help staring at the glass funeral carriage and the lonely coffin inside, wrapped up like a parcel in the Union flag. The jet-black horses attached to the carriage stamped their feet as if in sympathy. Six officers with bowed heads lined up outside the church ready to receive the coffin.

"The Battle of the Somme could be this country's downfall," one officer said to another in a high-pitched voice as the cart passed them.

The officer standing beside him laid a hand on his arm. "Shush, we are not allowed to talk of these things, Harold," he said anxiously. He looked up and caught Clara's eye. She glanced away and squeezed her hands together in her lap. Being in this town, surrounded by signs that the country was at war, reminded her of her home town in Kent. While there were still signs of war on the Earl's estate, at least she could escape to the hothouses and give her tired brain a rest from it all.

Robert flicked Kitty's reins hard and she trotted on, faster than before, away from the funeral and past a huge stone archway. "There is the Abbeygate," said Robert, following Clara's gaze through the archway to the formal gardens beyond, where people were walking, huddled up against the gusty wind. On the opposite side of the road a woman was half-running behind two small boys in tweed caps. One had his legs twisted around a hobby horse which had a red handkerchief tied around its neck, while the other was chasing him with a toy rifle. "Bang, bang," the boy with the gun yelled to the horse-riding boy. "You're killed." They were giggling as they ran along a cobbled street stretching up a hill. Clara stared at the street sign. *Abbeygate Street*. The location of the framemakers' shop. She brushed the tips of her fingers against the tapestry in her pocket, wondering how she was going to escape from Robert to visit it. She glanced at him. Robert was watching the small boys. The little brothers.

Clara curled her nails into her palms. "Where does your family live, Robert?"

Robert's fingers tightened on the reins. "I don't have any family," he said, his eyes sliding away from the little boys and towards Clara. His face was stony.

"Oh," said Clara. "I'm sorry…I thought…"

"There's nothing to be sorry about," said Robert sharply. "My parents are dead."

"So…you don't have any brothers or sisters?" A muscle in the side of Robert's face twitched. Clara held her breath.

"No," Robert said. He pushed his spectacles onto his nose and sniffed. "Sorry, Clara. I find it hard to speak of these things."

"Oh, I'm sorry. I didn't mean to pry," Clara said. Robert was doing his best to protect Will, but the worry of looking after his younger brother must be eating away at him.

The silence between them stretched until she thought it might snap. Robert's hands gripped the reins so tightly his knuckles reminded her of snow-capped mountains. Kitty rounded a corner, narrowly missing a man crossing the road with his yapping terrier.

"Hey, watch out!" the man shouted.

Robert ignored him. Clara bit down on her bottom lip. How could she make things better between them? "You're doing a good thing, organizing these fruits and vegetables for the hospital."

A flush stole onto Robert's cheeks. "Well, it was the Earl's idea, I can't take all of the credit," he muttered.

"Yes…but Mrs Gilbert was saying how proud she is of you, after your…disappointments." Clara clamped her mouth shut. She was prying again.

Robert rubbed his nose. The flush had mottled his neck, like a nettle rash. "The thing is, Clara – and you'll learn this when you are grown – you can get over some disappointments. But others stay with you, perhaps for ever."

Clara stared at Robert for a second, then looked away.

CHAPTER 23

Hospital Blues

"We're here," Robert said, bringing Kitty to a halt in a street just around the corner from the Abbeygate. His face seemed a little lighter as he hopped down from the cart and looped Kitty's reins around a lamp post. "Good girl," he murmured, stroking her mane. "We shan't be long."

Ivy coated the front of the three-storey hospital and crept over some of the windows too. The Union flag and the Red Cross flapped on the white flagpole – two flags Clara had grown to know well since the War had begun.

Robert and Clara unloaded the crates of vegetables and carried them to the entrance. A man wearing a blue shirt with too-short sleeves and baggy trousers was smoking near the doors. He leaned on wooden crutches. His right trouser leg was neatly folded at the knee; the lower half of his leg was missing.

Clara swallowed a gasp, her feet grinding to a halt, her eyes glued to where his leg once was. She heard Robert disappear inside. The crate Clara was holding tipped in her arms. Two parsnips and three carrots fell onto the pavement.

The man with one leg propped a crutch against the wall, and rested his cigarette and matches on the rim of a large plant pot next to him. "No pockets in these Hospital Blues," he said, gesturing to his outfit. "Can you imagine it?"

Clara stared at his odd-looking outfit. No pockets? How could a person be expected to travel through a day without them?

"You've got a good pair of pockets, I see," the man said, indicating Clara's apron. His voice was tinged with envy.

She glanced down and saw the tip of her envelope from the War Office was peeping out. By the time she looked up again, the man was bending awkwardly to pick up the fallen parsnips. "Oh, please. There is no need…" Clara began to say as the man picked them up and placed them carefully back in her crate.

"It's nice to be useful," he said, giving Clara a small smile.

"Yes, it is rather," said Clara, smiling back. "Well… thank you."

She waited as he bent again to pick up the carrots.

Robert strode out of the doors. His eyes skimmed over the man, to the crate in Clara's arms. "Mr Gilbert is expecting us back within the hour."

Clara gave him a small nod.

The man picked up his crutch and his cigarettes. Clara's eyes flickered to his leg again.

"It doesn't hurt me much, if that's what you're thinking," he said softly, following her gaze.

"Oh, no…I…" Clara felt a flash of heat rise up her neck.

"It's natural to be curious. And the docs here say it helps to talk about it. And now I've started talking, I can't seem to stop. Leg was blown clean off. Nurses in France saved my life. Proper angels they were."

Is that what had happened to Christopher? Is that what the letter from the War Office said? Clara looked at the man again and instead of seeing him, saw the dimple in Christopher's chin, the hair like Father's, which refused to lie flat unless he greased it. A leg that might or might not be there any more.

"This is the last of them," Clara heard Robert mutter as he walked past, his back stooped under the weight of the crates.

The man was still looking at her as if he wanted to talk. She should go and help Robert, but it would be rude to just walk away.

Clara cleared her throat. "Was it very awful? On the Front, I mean." The crate was making her arms ache. She placed it on the pavement and took a step closer to the man.

The man's eyes darkened. "You have family there?"

Clara nodded.

The man's eyes became glassy. He cleared his throat. "It's worse than what they say in the newspapers – which don't tell the whole truth. You couldn't understand it unless you'd been."

"Please. I would like to know," said Clara, clasping her hands together.

The man's Adam's apple bobbed in his throat. "The trenches are like a maze. Sometimes the fighting is so terrible that there's no time to bury the dead anywhere else. When it rains, the sides of the trenches collapse so people's legs and arms, and sometimes skulls, stick out."

Clara curled her toes in her boots to try and quell the sickness which had leaped into her stomach.

"The yellow mud gets everywhere. It fills your boots, jams the rifles and guns, makes you so cold you wouldn't think you could get any colder." The man rubbed his neck. "But it was the noises that got me. The air's thick with grenades and mortars. It's like ten explosions rolled into one. And as for the smells…"

"Charlie," said a nurse in a crisp white hat, sticking her head around the front door. "Are you bothering this young lady?"

"No…he wasn't. Not at all," said Clara. Although she was rather glad the nurse had appeared. She had not expected the man to go into quite so much detail. She had learned more from him in a few minutes than she had in all the months since her father returned from the Front. He had made it very clear he did not wish to speak of his experiences. Was this why?

The nurse ushered Charlie towards the door. He gave Clara a quick wave.

"Goodbye," Clara called. "And…good luck."

The man's cheeks cracked into a broad smile. He tipped his hand into a salute before disappearing through the doors.

When all of the vegetables had been dropped off at the kitchen storeroom – and the rosy-faced cook had kissed Robert on both cheeks to thank him for the Earl's generosity – they returned to the cart and Kitty.

Robert's eyes flickered to his watch. "I've a quick errand to run – at the post office. There's no need for you to come. I'll be ten minutes tops."

Kitty was still standing contently chewing on some parsnips Robert had dropped for her.

"Perhaps I could walk to the Abbeygate? Find a bakery and buy us a bun each for the journey back?" Clara asked.

Robert frowned. "Do you know where to go?"

Clara felt in her pocket for the folded tapestry. "I know it. It's just around the corner, back the way we came. I'll be quick."

Robert threw a concerned glance at Kitty, then gave Clara a quick, but serious nod. "Fine. But don't go telling Mr Gilbert. I promised not to let you out of my sight."

"You can trust me," Clara said, throwing him a broad smile.

Towards the end of the street she turned, and saw Robert still standing by Kitty, watching her. At the street corner she paused and looked back again. But this time Robert was striding off in the opposite direction with his collar pulled up, his shoulders hunched forward into the brisk autumn wind, a whirl of fallen leaves dancing in his wake.

CHAPTER 24

Abbeygate Street

Summers & Sons Framemakers was halfway up the cobbled street, sandwiched between a chemist, its window display full of jars of brightly-coloured liquids, and a bakery. Clara ignored the gurgle in her stomach elicited by the scent of freshly baked cinnamon-glazed Chelsea buns, making a mental note to buy three on the way back – for her, Robert and Will. The framemakers' shop bell jangled as Clara pushed the door open. She had half-walked, half-run all the way there, ignoring the curious gazes of afternoon shoppers, and she gathered her breath as she stood in the doorway. The maroon-painted walls were covered by a jigsaw of picture frames – delicate ones edged in silver, large wooden ones as big as a window, fancy gilt-edged frames which were thicker than the pictures they would eventually frame. "Hello, higgledy-piggledy puzzle wall," Clara said breathlessly.

The shopkeeper behind the counter was talking to a lady in a smart blue hat, explaining the differences between two small frames, which looked exactly the same to Clara. It seemed the lady thought so too, for she said she could not decide and would return the following week. The shopkeeper sighed and placed the frames under the counter as the lady brushed past Clara and left, the doorbell jangling a quick goodbye.

The shopkeeper glanced up at Clara. "Can I help you?" His white catlike whiskers wiggled as he spoke. He reminded Clara a little of Neptune.

Clara stepped closer to the counter. "You framed a tapestry for Mrs Gilbert, I mean, my aunt."

The shopkeeper tilted his head. "Is there a problem with it?"

Clara rubbed her bottom lip. "There was an accident. The frame broke." She pulled the folded tapestry from her pocket and placed it on the counter. She stood back and watched the shopkeeper's face as he smoothed it out and studied it.

"Well," he said, "that's a very fine-looking pineapple. The fabric will need to be stretched before it can be reframed though."

"Oh. Will that take long?" Clara asked.

"A day or so. It's not urgent?"

Clara dipped her head and stared at her scuffed boots. "I think it may be."

"Ah, I see," said the shopkeeper. Clara looked up. He was giving her a friendly smile, as if he understood exactly what type of emergency it was. "When I was small I broke one of my father's clay pipes, his favourite. A chimney sweep lived next door. I carried his brushes every day after school until I had enough money to replace it."

"I have some money," Clara said. "My parents gave it to me for emergencies."

"Hmm. Did they now? And you think this might be one?" the shopkeeper asked, smoothing his moustache.

Clara gave him a small nod.

The shopkeeper pulled a large brown ledger from beneath the counter. "You don't happen to remember the date on the back of the frame?"

"1914," said Clara quickly.

"And the name was Gilbert, you say?"

"Mrs Elizabeth Gilbert," replied Clara, nibbling on a thumbnail.

The man flicked through the ledger, running a forefinger down the pages lined with perfect handwriting. "Here we are," he said, jabbing his finger at a page. "Yes, I have all the measurements. He chose cherrywood. A good choice. Oh, there was to be an inscription on the front of the frame, but your uncle changed his mind."

"My uncle?" said Clara, wrinkling her nose.

"Yes. Mr Gilbert ordered the frame."

Clara held onto the countertop. "What was it to say?"

The man squinted. "Deep peace of the quiet earth." He swallowed, rubbed his jaw.

Clara frowned. It sounded rather gloomy, but also rather nice. It fitted the tapestry quite well, for pineapples did grow peacefully in the soil. She had a sudden longing to be back in the hothouses with Will, where the air was warm and still and sweet.

"Would you like the inscription on a brass plate?" the shopkeeper asked, his pen poised over the ledger. "It will cost a little more. I imagine that's why your uncle decided against it."

Deep peace of the quiet earth.

"That would be lovely," said Clara. "But I need to check I have enough money first." She pulled her purse from her pocket and tipped the contents onto the counter.

The shopkeeper quickly counted the coins and glanced at the ledger again. He tapped a finger on his chin, then pushed half of the coins back across the counter to Clara. "You have more than enough," he said firmly. "Shall I send the package to Gardener's Cottage, addressed to…Mrs Gilbert?"

"Yes, please," said Clara, sweeping the leftover coins back into her purse and pushing it into her pocket.

She picked up the piece of paper that had tumbled out with the coins and handed it to him. "Please can you put this behind the tapestry?"

The shopkeeper took it from her and gave her a quick nod, as if it was an everyday occurrence to be asked to place pieces of paper bearing the word *Maestro* behind replacement tapestry frames.

She walked to the door, but then paused and turned, watching the shopkeeper smoothing out the tapestry. "I don't suppose there is any chance at all it will be ready by tomorrow? You see…my aunt doesn't know I've brought it into town and…"

The shopkeeper looked up and smiled another crinkly smile, which was a little sadder than the first and didn't quite reach his eyes. "Not much call for framing at the moment, what with the War. Both of my sons are at the Front. Had no news of them for a while. Well, we get the odd letter, but most of the detail is censored. You know how it is."

Clara gave a serious nod, thinking of the shop sign swinging outside. *Summers & Sons.* She desperately hoped his sons would return.

"I'll see what I can do about getting this tapestry reframed quickly. We can't have you getting into trouble, can we?" the shopkeeper said.

Clara smiled her thanks, giving the wall of picture frames a final glance on her way out. It was curious that Mr Gilbert had ordered the frame. Surely, having sewn the tapestry, Mrs Gilbert would have wanted a say in the final choice? But then again, perhaps it had been a surprise, for her birthday or Christmas. Whatever the reason, Clara dearly hoped that paying for the brass inscription plate would at least halfway make up for her trespassing in their bedroom and breaking a precious thing which did not belong to her.

CHAPTER 25

Parcel for Will

After helping the stable boy clean the cart and bed down Kitty in her stable, Clara and Robert walked back down the hill to the gardens. Clara pushed the final piece of her Chelsea bun into her mouth, her gums aching at the sugary sweetness.

"Thanks for the bun, Clara," Robert said, licking a shred of lemon peel from his thumb.

Clara smiled. Robert had been surly and pale-faced when she had returned from the framemakers' shop, but as they made their way out of the town, his shoulders had seemed to relax and he had begun to chat. He had become quite animated as he spoke of the poor wheat harvest that year, how he was concerned that there may be food shortages soon and perhaps even rationing. Clara had thought of the Gilberts' pantry, loaded with jars of jams, pickles and chutneys. Perhaps she would ask to take a few home with her – if she ever went home…

Having left Robert with Mr Gilbert outside The Bothy, Clara opened the door to the cottage. A note from Mrs Gilbert was on the sideboard, saying that she would be working late at the Big House. It was an opportunity she could not ignore.

The bun Clara had eaten sat heavy in her stomach as she traipsed upstairs and unhooked the key to the locked room from behind the Gilberts' bed. She should not be trespassing in the Gilberts' room again. She most certainly should not be taking keys and unlocking doors and reading letters which did not belong to her. But what if other letters had arrived, ones that *did* belong to her? She had been at the cottage for over a week and there had been no word from her mother, no answers to the letters she had written and asked Mrs Gilbert to post. Clara walked to the bureau and picked up the envelope on top of the pile. Just like last time there was no name or address on the front. Was this the same letter she had already read, or could it be a new one? She slipped out the sheaf of paper and began to read.

October 1916

My Dearest,

Time is passing so quickly. The days are shortening and Alfred has thrown himself into the gardens — he is obsessed with them. He is often at work with his spade and fork before sunrise and does not return until teatime. Afterwards we sit by the fire, barely speaking as we stare into the flames, both wishing for the same thing I am sure — to be free. Oh, to hear your laugh! What joy that would bring me. Maybe tonight, when I creep through the gardens while everyone sleeps, I will see you. I will be waiting as usual, near our favourite pineapple house.

Your fondest,

Lizzy

Clara stared hard at the words, willing them to reveal their secrets. Mrs Gilbert had admitted in her letter that she was creeping around the gardens and visiting the hothouses. As much as Clara did not want to believe it, could Will's theory that the Gilberts were stealing the pineapples be right? And wasn't it a little peculiar that Mrs Gilbert was not specifically dating her letters? Did she have any intention of addressing them and posting them? Carefully pushing the letter back into its envelope, she placed it back on top of the pile, ensuring it rested at a slight angle, just as she had found it.

That evening Will's face was paler than usual, his eyes red-rimmed, when Clara met him at the boiler house. "Robert came to see me," he said, his voice cracked and low. He picked up a lump of coal and threw it at the wall. It shattered into tiny pieces.

Clara's tongue felt too large for her mouth. Had she made Robert suspicious by questioning him about his family on their way into town earlier?

"Father's regiment have returned his uniform and his personal items." Will slumped on the blanket next to Clara.

"Oh," said Clara, handing him the bun she had bought in town. Will didn't even look inside the paper bag, just placed it on the blanket beside him. Clara picked at the skin around her thumbnail. Was that why Robert's cheeks had been pinched and pale earlier on? He must have been to collect their father's things from the post office. "What will you do with them?" She hugged her knees to her chest. Despite the warmth from the furnace, cold seeped through her bones, making her shudder.

"I think…" He paused. "Robert and I think they should be buried."

The boiler spat and hissed.

Clara turned and looked at Will in surprise, remembering the funeral she had seen in town earlier that day. "In a churchyard?"

"No," said Will wearily. "That wouldn't be allowed."

"Where then?"

"Father and I came to visit Robert, soon after he'd started working here. It was springtime. The trees were full of birdsong. Bulbs were pushing up through the soil. Everything was fresh and new, like a drawing that had just been finished."

Clara's throat ached. For the things Will had just told her. For the loss of his father. For the things that might have happened to her own brother that she was still not brave enough to face.

Will reached behind him for a cushion-sized parcel wrapped in brown paper and string. He placed it on his lap and dragged in a breath. "Do you want to see?" he asked.

Clara felt her head nod. The anxiety in her stomach grew larger, like a rolling snowball. She did not know what she had imagined, but it wasn't for their father's possessions to be sent like a normal parcel through the post. Surely there should have been a trumpet playing, a parade, a more fitting acknowledgement that he gave his life for his country than just a parcel wrapped in brown paper?

Will pulled on the string; folded back the paper. The olive-green uniform was similar to her father's, and to the one Christopher had been wearing when he had left home, walking proudly down the street, his back straight, his eyes dancing and ready for the adventures to come. As Will unfolded the fabric, Clara drew in a sharp breath. The left arm of the jacket had been roughly cut away. A dark brown stain covered the shoulder. *Blood.* Will had told her the telegram informing them of their father's death had said it had been quick and painless and that he had not suffered. But how could any death caused by war be painless? A wave of dizziness washed over Clara as Will brought the jacket close to his face. He drew in a deep breath through his nose. "It smells…musty. Not of him," he said in a flat voice.

Clara placed a hand on Will's arm, tears burning her throat.

187

"What do you think happens when we die?" Will asked quietly.

Clara pulled away her hand and closed her eyes for a second. The room was spinning, like she was on a merry-go-round at the town fair. When she opened them again the first thing she saw was Will's notebook, lying open. She picked it up, tracing a finger over a drawing of a pineapple so detailed she could see the individual quilts and spikes. She drew in a deep steadying breath. "I think it might be like...falling into the gaps between pictures on a page," she said slowly. "Just not...there any more."

Will pressed the jacket to his cheek. "I like that," he said. His face was flushed, his eyes watery. He sniffed and looked at the ceiling.

"Your father would have been proud of you, Will," Clara said softly.

"You think?"

Clara nodded. "Your drawings of the gardens, your plans for the future. He would have liked hearing about those."

A flash of embarrassment crossed Will's face, but a small smile also crinkled the corners of his mouth. "Would you...come with me, to bury Father's uniform, tonight?"

Clara frowned. "What about Robert?"

Will's lips thinned. "He won't come. Told me he couldn't face it."

"But…he's your brother."

Will shook his head. "He finds these things…hard."

Clara rubbed at a coal stain on her apron, remembering her conversation with Robert as the horse and cart jolted them into town. He *was* finding things difficult, that much she could see. But not to want to be there for your own brother at a time like this was hard to understand.

Will carefully rewrapped the uniform. "I know you find things hard too, Clara. But you should open the letter from the War Office. There's nothing scarier than not knowing the truth," he said sadly.

Clara pressed her lips together, picked up a piece of fallen coal and clasped it in her hand. Will was right. She must pluck up the courage and open the letter. But maybe tomorrow would be the day her mother would contact Mrs Gilbert. Perhaps she would send for Clara to come home and she would be able to thrust the letter into her mother's make-things-better fingers and she would not have to make any decision at all.

CHAPTER 26

Being Brave

It was past midnight. The moon was almost full, the sky clear and cold, and the sound of rifle fire seemed closer than usual. Clara pulled her shawl around her shoulders and shivered. "Are you sure the Regiment aren't practising in the woods?" she whispered to Will. Straying beyond the gardens when soldiers were firing their rifles did seem rather foolish.

"Not the part we're going to," Will replied, hugging the parcel containing his father's things close to his chest.

As they wound their way around the garden to a door in the east wall which led to the woods, the shovel Clara was carrying clanked painfully against her shins.

Will pushed open the door and gestured for Clara to go ahead. Stepping forward, her right boot sank into something soft (and very un-grass-like). She bent down, her breath hitching in her throat when she saw what it was. A squished boot-imprinted mandarin.

"Goodness, look," she whispered to Will, picking up the pulpy mess. A dribble of juice ran down her wrist. As she stood up, she noticed two small, stone, cupid statues on plinths, one on either side of the door. The first cupid was empty-handed, but in the right palm of the second statue rested another mandarin. The one she had trodden on had probably rolled off the first statue's hand, maybe helped by a puff of wind.

Will did not respond, just clutched his father's parcel closer to his chest as he stared at the fruit. Clara carefully placed the squished mandarin back where it had fallen from and wiped her fingers on her apron. Now was not the time to wonder why this fruit was being deliberately left in the gardens – for she was sure that it was. Now was the time to help Will.

Neither of them spoke as their feet cracked over twigs, brushed through nettles and around brambles.

"Here," Will said, after Clara had counted they had walked past seventy-six trees of varying sizes and shapes. Breath steamed from their lips as they stood in a small clearing, tree stumps perching on the soil like giant's feet. Clara leaned the shovel against one of the stumps, which was overgrown with lichen. Will placed the parcel on another and then picked up the shovel.

"Snowdrops grow here in the spring. Crocuses too. Father loved them," Will said.

A snake of cold air wriggled down the neck of Clara's coat. She pushed autumn away, instead imagining the sun dappling through the trees, the earthy smell of green shoots pushing through the soil. Life beginning all over again.

Will began to dig, shovelling earth over his shoulder. He paused, took off his jacket and wiped his brow, a cough racking his chest. Clara took the jacket from him and folded it over her arm.

The hole Will was digging grew deeper, plenty large enough for the parcel. Lines of sweat trickled down his face. He coughed again and wiped his nose with the back of his hand.

Distant rifle fire echoed through the trees. Will was right, the Regiment were practising in a different part of the woods tonight, but the sharp staccato bursts still dried Clara's mouth and caused her hands to ball into fists. Were these the sounds that Will's father had heard as he died, the sounds her father and brother had grown accustomed to? She did her best to push the thoughts away. "I think it's big enough, Will," Clara whispered. But the chink of the metal through the soil and the sound of Will's laboured breathing smothered her words.

Will grunted, flinging soil over his shoulder as the hole grew bigger still.

Clara took a step forward. "It's done, Will," she said, louder this time.

Still Will continued to dig. He stood in the hole, his legs swallowed by the heap of earth, so he seemed only half the person he was.

"Will," Clara said urgently.

Will paused, then glanced at Clara as if he had forgotten she was there. "Yes," he said in a strangled voice. He looked down at the hole. He looked at the parcel. "You'd best hand it to me."

Clara carefully picked up the package and passed it to him.

Will hugged it to his chest one more time. He dipped his chin and sucked in a deep breath. A huge cough made his body shake.

Robert should be here, to help his brother, Clara thought. *Will should not be doing this alone.* But Robert wasn't there, and she was. Clara stepped forward, her boots sinking into the soil. She laid her hands over Will's. Very gently, she guided the parcel towards the hole. They crouched beside one another, their hands still joined. Will's fingers were icy and encrusted with mud. But that did not matter one jot to Clara. She pressed the parcel into the soil until her own nails, fingers and hands were as dirty as his. "Goodbye," Clara whispered.

Will began to tremble, like someone had taken hold of his body and was giving it a jolly good shake. He wiped his nose again, then sprang to his feet and began to shovel soil on top of the parcel until all traces of the brown paper were hidden.

Clara forced her eyes to stay fixed on Will's stony face, even though a tiny part of her wanted to turn away, run away – from the woods, from the buried uniform stained with blood, from the tears sliding down his cheeks.

It was done. Will dropped the shovel to the ground. He wrapped his arms around his middle and bent forward as if he had a pain in his side.

Clara folded her arms around her own body. Trekking over snowy mountains, floating through the air high above the world in a balloon – that took a certain kind of bravery. But this was a different kind of bravery, a type Clara had never seen before and very much hoped she would never have to see again.

CHAPTER 27

The Basket

October 1916

My Dearest,

Do you remember the first time you tasted a home-grown pineapple from the hothouse? How sweet the yellow flesh was, so different to the imported pineapples that arrive salt-weathered and sour at the London docks. The sheer delight on your face!

It takes me much effort to rise in the mornings now. I find my mind drifting to you while I work, directing the scullery maids to blacken the hearths and lay the fires at the Big House. I have little appetite to clean my own cottage. Alfred has mentioned more than once the lacelike cobwebs hanging in the corners, the balls of dust

*drifting under the bed like silent mice. He is suspicious,
I think, but I am beyond caring. All I wish is for us to
be together, my dear.
Your fondest,
Lizzy*

Clara slid the letter into the envelope. It was as if the
letters were magnetized, drawing her into the room to
read them despite the risk of being caught. Mrs Gilbert
must have been in the room writing her secret letters
while Clara had been helping Will bury his father's things
the night before. She checked each drawer of the bureau
again for letters from her mother. There were none.

Locking the door, Clara returned the key to the
Gilberts' bedroom and ran down the stairs, taking
the steps two at a time. Hurling open the door to the
gardens, she pulled in a breath of early afternoon
autumn air, which was thinner and chillier than it had
been. She walked quickly down the slope towards the
boiler house. She wondered what Will was doing.
Sleeping? Stoking the boiler? Drawing in his notebook?
The way he spoke about the pineapples and the
hothouses was so tender, like they were his family.
Maybe they were now.

197

Mr Gilbert was talking to Robert under the apple trees. He was gesticulating, pointing at the hothouses. Clara skirted through the trees until she was standing near enough to hear what was being said.

"Two, you say?" said Robert.

"Yes, and a dozen peaches as well. The Earl will want the police involved," said Mr Gilbert firmly.

"Not yet," said Robert quickly. "I've been keeping watch. I'll stay up tonight, try and catch them. They're bound to try again."

"Are you sure about that?" Mr Gilbert asked curtly.

"I'm…not sure what you mean," said Robert.

"*Have* you been watching the hothouses? By all accounts you were tucked up in your bed early last night, snoring the place down."

A fly buzzed around Clara's head. She swatted it away.

"The work in the gardens is tiring," Robert said eventually. His voice was thin, edged with guilt.

"Course it is, lad. There's a war on, which means more work for everyone. And on top of that, a thief is ransacking the Earl's hothouses," Mr Gilbert said wearily.

"I'm sorry…"

Clara's legs felt like jelly. More fruit had been taken, and it had happened when they were not keeping watch. Coming back from the woods the previous night, Will had been shaky, his feet stumbling over every branch, around every bush. Clara had persuaded him to return to the boiler house to sleep, rather than keep watch in the hothouse.

She had been exhausted too. It had been an odd kind of tiredness, which had made her limbs feel heavy and caused her to collapse into bed as soon as she got back to her room, sleep engulfing her the instant her head touched the pillow. As usual she had left her bedroom window open, but nothing and no one had woken her. No nightmare, or creak of a hothouse door or footsteps thudding across the grass; no voices carried in by the breeze. Clara itched to speak with Will.

She rested a hand on the trunk of a gnarly apple tree; laid her cheek against the rough bark.

"I promised a basket of apples to the Regiment," Mr Gilbert said, reaching up and picking a couple of apples and placing them in a barrow. "Can you take them?"

"As you said, there's a lot to do here," Robert replied in a clipped voice.

There was a pause. Mr Gilbert picked another apple

and dropped it into the barrow. "The army also has a lot to do, keeping us safe."

Robert kicked hard at a fallen apple with the toe of his boot; it split into several pieces. Mr Gilbert picked up his spade, flung it over his shoulder and strode off to the far side of the gardens.

An idea was simmering in Clara's head. A stack of wicker baskets leaned against the brick wall nearby. Uncurling herself from the tree, Clara walked across and picked one up, looping it over her arm. The breeze ruffled the leaves above her head and the apples bobbed and bounced. Robert was looking at her. She ignored him, reached up to one of the lower branches, chose an apple flushed with pink and twisted. It came away in her hand. She placed it in the basket, then carried on twisting and picking until the basket was half-filled.

Robert wandered over and glanced into the basket. "You're picking a good crop there," he said, leaning against a tree. His eyes looked pink, his top lip beaded with sweat.

"I thought you might need some help," said Clara.

"There's so much to do," said Robert. "Sometimes too much." He took off his glasses, pulled a handkerchief from his pocket and blew his nose, then wiped his face.

A pang of sympathy tightened Clara's jaw. Poor Robert. Mr Gilbert was working him very hard. All the worry he had about hiding Will and finding them somewhere to live – it must be so very wearing. "I can help...would you like me to pick more apples?"

Robert pushed his handkerchief into his pocket and glanced at Mr Gilbert, who was digging a planting bed along the back wall. "I need to take some apples to the Regiment's camp."

"I could take them," Clara said eagerly – maybe too eagerly. "I have nothing else to do," she added with a shrug.

Robert scratched his chin. "It would be a help. I have to ready another cartload of vegetables for the hospital and tend to the leeks. There just aren't enough hours in the day."

"No, there really aren't," replied Clara, pressing her boots into the grass. "Don't worry. I'll take the apples and be back before you know it."

"You really are helpful, aren't you?" said Robert thoughtfully.

Clara felt his eyes on her like the prickle of a beetle walking up her arm. She needed to be careful not to make him suspicious. She forced her lips into a bright smile and pushed away the tinge of unease in her gut. Taking the apples to the Regiment *would* help Robert, but (maybe a little selfishly) she hoped it would help *her* more.

When Will heard that more fruit had been taken, he was bound to bring up his theory again that Mrs Gilbert was the thief. When he spoke like that, his voice changed, became harder, and it made Clara's head ache. If she could visit the Regiment's camp, maybe she could find Thomas the soldier and ask him what had been in the basket Mrs Gilbert had given him. She felt certain that Mrs Gilbert had nothing to do with the stolen pineapples, and while she and her aunt did not get on the way she had hoped, it was important to prove this to Will, so they could concentrate on finding the real culprit.

CHAPTER 28

A Dreadful Business

The trees rustled and murmured in the stiff wind; sunlight flickered through the branches which were waving goodbye to their leaves for another year. Crows bustled in the sky like black handkerchiefs, as the sound of voices filtered from where the woodland path fanned out onto open fields. Two men were sitting on a farm gate, swinging back and forth. They paused when they saw Clara, one of them raising a hand in greeting. As she approached them she trod over discarded cigarette ends and heavy boot-prints.

The Regiment's tents were in rows, like sheets on washing lines. Pegged to the tent ropes were items of clothing – socks and men's underwear, which made

Clara want to look in the opposite direction. In front of the tents and nearest to the woods was a long trestle table, with two benches on either side. To the right of this was another larger tent, where a spiral of smoke was rising.

One of the men jumped down from the gate and walked towards her. He was chewing on a blade of grass. "Hello. What do you have there?"

Clara stared at his olive-green trousers, his undone jacket. She felt her pulse quicken. His uniform was similar to Christopher's. She placed the basket on the ground and massaged her aching arm. "Apples…for… Cook," she said. "From the head gardener."

"The mess tent is over there," the soldier said with a friendly smile, pointing to the spiralling smoke. "They look good." He reached into the basket and picked up an apple, rubbing it on his sleeve before taking a huge bite from it. "We appreciate everything the Earl's doing for us. It's good to eat well," he said with his mouth full.

Clara picked the basket up again and glanced over at the other tents. "I'm also looking for…Thomas."

"Which one? There are several Thomases here."

"The tall one…with the moustache," said Clara.

"Oh yes. And what would you be wanting with him?" the soldier asked lightly.

Clara felt a flush crawl up her neck and spill onto her cheeks.

"Is it a message – from Elizabeth?" he asked.

Clara stared at him. He knew Thomas had been meeting her aunt? The tents' doors were flapping like eager ears.

The soldier took another bite of the apple and crunched it slowly. "You can pass a message onto me if you like. I'll tell him when he returns from training."

"Um," said Clara, racking her brains. "It's nothing. I'd better deliver these apples. I need to be getting back. Mr Gilbert is expecting me."

The soldier's eyes narrowed and he nodded. "Such a pity. Dreadful business. Hope they can resolve it before we move out to the Front."

The soldier was talking in riddles. What dreadful business did he mean? Clara filed the information in her brain to take out and examine later, then brushed past the soldier and headed towards the mess tent.

"Hello," Clara said cautiously, peering under the canvas flap. "Is anyone there?" The tent was empty of people but filled with provisions. A trestle table was weighed down with loaves of bread and tins of food. Another table was stacked with metal plates, mugs and cooking equipment.

Something under the first table caught her eye – a basket, the same as the one Mrs Gilbert had been carrying. It was covered by the same cloth too. Clara's breath caught in her throat. Setting the apple basket down, she crouched. Wind flapped the canvas of the tent in and out, in and out. It seemed to be saying, *Look inside, look inside.*

She lifted the cloth, reached in and pulled out a skinny leek. Next to the leeks were a handful of potatoes and carrots and some purple beets. She sat back on her heels, a shiver of relief running through her that she hadn't found a basket loaded with pineapples and peaches – Mrs Gilbert was not the thief.

"What have we here?" asked a voice from behind her.

Clara stood up, blood rushing to her head. A stocky man in a white overall with a spoon in his hand was staring at her.

"Apple delivery," Clara said.

The man's face cracked into a broad smile. He

opened his arms as if to hug her and Clara shrank back into the tent. "Marvellous! Apple sauce for pudding. You can tell that head gardener the soldiers would gladly kiss his boots if he came to visit."

Cook's laugh was infectious and she smiled too. Kissing Mr Gilbert's boots. Now that would be a sight to see.

"Clara? Is that you?"

Clara paused at the Gilberts' bedroom door, which was ajar. Mrs Gilbert was sitting on the edge of her bed, her back rod-straight. Her hands were gripping a picture frame that was lying on her lap.

She looked up. "Come in, will you?"

Clara tentatively pushed the door open and stepped inside.

"Goodness. Whatever have you been doing? You look...quite worn out. And in need of a bath."

Clara glanced down at her mud-tinged apron; tucked her tangled hair behind her ears. "I've been delivering apples to the Regiment," she said.

"That's good. They're short of food," Mrs Gilbert said with a small smile.

But if Mr Gilbert is sending the Regiment food with the Earl's approval, why are you giving vegetables to Thomas when everyone is asleep? What is the dreadful business the soldier said you and Thomas must try to resolve?

"Come in, then," Mrs Gilbert said, beckoning her forward.

Clara pushed the thoughts to one side and glanced at the frame on Mrs Gilbert's lap. It was the pineapple tapestry. Mr Summers had been as good as his word, and mended and delivered it even more quickly than she'd thought possible. The brass plate and inscription glinted in the light. *Deep peace of the quiet earth*.

"Did you choose this?" Mrs Gilbert ran her finger over the plate, her fingers lingering on each word.

"Mr Gilbert did – the first time it was framed," Clara said.

Mrs Gilbert's lips wobbled.

Clara clasped her hands behind her back – they suddenly felt rather sweaty.

Mrs Gilbert stood up, walked to the head of the bed and hung the frame on the wall. She took a handkerchief from her pocket and gave the brass plate a quick polish.

"Thank you," she said, turning to Clara.

Clara's cheeks felt hot.

Mrs Gilbert stepped across the room in her stockinged feet and placed her hands on Clara's shoulders.

Clara stiffened in surprise. This was the closest she had been to Mrs Gilbert since she arrived – apart from the unfortunate hair incident. Without warning, her aunt pulled her into a hug. It was not a warm and motherly one, smelling of fresh linen cupboards or strawberries. This hug smelled of furniture polish, and reminded her more of a sad shoe brush with worn, wiry bristles. But Clara had not been hugged for so long that she felt her body begin to betray her and relax into Mrs Gilbert's arms. Mrs Gilbert rested her chin on Clara's head for a second and took a long slow breath.

The slap. The hidden letters. Will. Father. Everything went through her mind.

But she must not be swayed by Mrs Gilbert's unexpected burst of softness. Clara pulled out of her grasp, turned on her heel and ran from the room.

"Clara!" Mrs Gilbert called.

Clara ignored her, ran up the stairs to her bedroom and slammed the door shut, standing with her back to it. She scrunched her eyes shut and pressed her fingers into them until she saw wavy black shapes, and the memory of Mrs Gilbert's hug faded into nothing.

CHAPTER 29

The Thief

It was after midnight. A drip of condensation from the glass roof of the pineapple house plopped onto the concrete near Clara's right boot. She reached forward and smudged it with her thumb, thinking about what Will had just told her. He had found another mandarin by the lake that evening, just before an autumn mist had begun to smother the gardens in an opaque cloak.

"Maybe someone is playing a prank, leaving this fruit for us to find," Will whispered. He had agreed with Clara's theory that the fruit was being left deliberately, but neither of them could imagine who would do such a thing. "Maybe it's one of the young under-gardeners?" he suggested.

"But you've checked the hothouse and you say no mandarins have been taken," said Clara.

"Maybe they come from somewhere else – the grocer's in town?" Will said with a shrug.

Clara wrinkled her nose. A garden full to the brim with fruit and the mandarins were being bought from a shop? She thought that very unlikely indeed. Anyway, why would a gardener risk losing his job over a silly prank?

"If we catch Mrs Gilbert tonight, then what will you do?" Will asked, changing the subject.

"I told you that the basket I found at the Regiment's camp contained vegetables from the gardens. You can't *still* think my aunt has something to do with the thieving? It's almost like…you *want* her to be responsible," Clara whispered, a flash of irritation tightening her jaw.

It was Will's turn to wrinkle his nose. He picked up a small stone and threw it at a plant pot. It dinged off the side and rolled onto the pathway separating the pineapple plants.

Hunching beneath the bench was making Clara's neck ache. "It's just…the Gilberts are family," she said, kneading at the pain with her fingers.

"And there's nothing more important than family," said Will in a small and rather lost voice.

Clara shifted a little closer to Will until their knees were nudging. "I've been away from home for so long, that when I think about my family it's hard to remember them properly. I wonder if this is what it was like for Father and Christopher when they went away to fight?"

Will glanced at her, seemed to be thinking about this. "Open the letter from the War Office, Clara. You need to know what it says, for your sake and for your parents'."

Clara dragged in a deep breath of warm, sweet air. At home she had lived alongside the War. It was real, but also at arm's length. Father's tight-lipped refusal to talk about his experiences on the Front. Mother's refusal to read the newspapers. This sometimes made it feel like they were living in a bubble, protected from the worst the War could throw at them. Here it was different. Burying Will's father's things. The soldier at the hospital with his injuries. The Regiment's camp on the edge of the woods and the nightly rifle fire. Mr Gilbert's stories of Zeppelins dropping bombs on nearby Norfolk. This war was like a mole, burying and tunnelling into her, popping up for air and leaving its mark. "Maybe," said Clara.

"Maybe yes, or maybe no? You're braver than you know. You need to stop worrying that you're not." Will grasped Clara's hand and gave it a firm squeeze. Wind licked the windowpanes, shivered from one to another like a round of applause. He gave her a look that she could not interpret, a sad look that made his face seem smaller, as if he was cast adrift from her, the hothouse and his beloved pineapples.

Clara squeezed his hand back.

"Shhh," hissed Will suddenly. His body had stiffened. He dropped her hand.

There were footsteps outside. But they were not the tiny footsteps of a night-time creature on the hunt for food.

The moisture in Clara's mouth vanished. Will's eyes were bright and excited in the dim light, his hands clenched on his knees. The footsteps travelled the length of the hothouse, then paused at the entrance. Clara felt like she had forgotten how to breathe. The feet trod softly down the steps. The door handle turned. Clara slunk back beneath the bench, but Will was leaning forward, peering at the door.

The footsteps were stealthy, not like the footsteps of someone who had a right to be walking inside the hothouse, caring for the fruits. Clara felt sure these were the footsteps of a person who meant to do them harm. She dug her nails into her palms.

A hot-water pipe gurgled. Clara swallowed the dryness in her throat. The feet were walking along the narrow path between the planting beds, growing closer, and closer still. Clara blinked. Blinked again. Even though it was dark, she had seen enough boots to know the ones now standing in front of the bench were men's army boots. The man's breaths were fairy-light and even, not at all how Clara had imagined a thief's breaths would sound. He turned and leaned against the bench, crossing his legs at the ankles.

Clara bit her lip as she watched Will reach out until there was less than a pin's space between his hands and the man's calves. Then, with a grunt, he lurched forward and grabbed the man's legs.

A noise came from the man's throat – a gurgle of shock and pain as he twisted and fell to the ground with a heavy thump.

Will scrabbled out from under the bench and Clara followed, her knees scraping on the rough paving. She smothered a gasp as she looked down into the shadows.

It was Mrs Gilbert's soldier-friend, Thomas.

Will turned and gave her a broad grin. *Told you so,* his eyes were saying.

There was a low scuffling noise behind Will. Clara opened her mouth to shout to him, but she was too late. Thomas had sprung to his feet and was gripping Will's shoulder. Will wriggled and squirmed. "Got you," Thomas said through gritted teeth.

In her panic, Clara grabbed onto the bench to steady herself and her fingers brushed against something small and wooden. It was the handle of a small gardening trowel. She picked it up, lifted it above her head and stared at Thomas, who now had his back to her as he struggled with Will. Clara flung the trowel towards the back of the hothouse, where it clattered on the ground.

"What the...?" Thomas muttered, momentarily loosening his grip on Will.

Clara turned and ran from the hothouse, up the steps and out into the mist. She could hear Will's footsteps close behind, then he was shooting past her like a hare. Clara swung around the left side of the hothouse, but Will was running in the opposite direction, up the slope towards the orchard, a cough hacking from his lungs. Thomas's feet were thudding on the grass, chasing Will.

Clara stared out into the mist, droplets of water clinging to her hair and cheeks, her breaths ragged in her throat. The gardens were eerily quiet, as if shocked into silence by the night's events. She didn't think Thomas had seen her face, but he knew that Will hadn't been alone. She needed to hide before he came looking for her. The thief knew they were on to him.

CHAPTER 30

Locked Up

Clara pulled open the large glass door to the Earl's summer house, shutting it quietly behind her. The warmth untied some of the knots in her tired muscles as she weaved around the white wicker chairs and past the mandarin trees in their giant terracotta pots. She tripped over two butterfly nets lying on the floor near the wall. Perhaps they belonged to the girls who had seen her sitting in the wild flowers. They were most likely fast asleep, dreaming about pretty dresses and lovely things. If they were here now, what would they make of her, hiding in a summer house (where she had no business hiding) from a pineapple thief?

Huddling behind the largest of the potted trees,

Clara watched the moonlight hit the chandelier above her, which was throwing beads of light along the walls, and listened to the distant rattle of gunfire. Her brain was a mess of thoughts, like a baby's scribbled drawing. Will was right – Thomas had been taking the fruit. But did Mrs Gilbert know? And where was Will now? He was fast, had speed on his side. But he was up against a trained soldier who had been taught to hurt and kill. If Thomas did catch Will, would he be held captive and bound so that he could not yell for help?

Clara dragged in a deep breath of citrusy air. She leaned forward and stroked a leaf on the mandarin tree. The tree did not have as many fruits as those in the hothouse. Maybe they did not grow as well here. She would ask Will. If she ever saw him again.

Tick-tick-tick-tick said the hot-water pipes. They were singing her a gentle tune, one that rolled wave after wave of tiredness through her body. Clara rubbed her eyes. She would check the boiler house in a couple of hours, just before dawn, to see if Will had returned. Until then she needed to stay hidden out of sight, in case Thomas returned.

"Clara? Clara?" The voice was insistent and nagging at the edge of her hearing.

Clara jerked awake, her heart thudding against her ribs.

Robert was kneeling in front of her. A lit oil lamp was on the floor next to him, although he barely needed it. The huge windows of the summer house framed the pink-tinged sky.

Clara scrabbled to her feet and rubbed her eyes.

"What in heaven's name are you doing in here? Folks have been looking for you," Robert said. His face was pale, the skin under his eyes as dark as bruises.

Clara glanced at her watch. It was just after 7 a.m. How could she have let herself fall asleep?

"Come on, we'd best let them know you're safe," Robert said, picking up the lamp.

Clara followed him out of the summer house, around the edges of the wall, until they came to the steps which led to the boiler house. The door at the foot of the steps was flung wide open.

Bile rose in Clara's throat. Will had not come back. "Wait," she said, planting her boots on the dewy grass.

Robert turned.

Clara's hands were clammy. She pulled the sleeves of her cardigan around her fingers.

Robert's cheeks were ice-white.

"It's about…Will," Clara said. She squeezed the wool between her fingers, hoping that Will would forgive her for breaking her promise.

Robert's eyes flickered to hers and then away again. The muscles in his jaw tensed.

Clara took a deep breath. "I met him in the gardens."

Robert's jaw twitched.

"We know that fruit has been stolen from the hothouses. We've been keeping watch for the thief. Last night…while we were watching, the thief came – Thomas. He chased after Will."

Robert massaged his throat.

Clara shifted from foot to foot. Why wasn't he leaping about, his eyes widening in horror? She glanced again at the entrance to the boiler house. Robert's eyes followed hers.

"I don't think Will came back to the boiler house last night. I think Thomas has caught him – maybe he's keeping him somewhere."

"He's been caught alright," Robert said with a sniff, pushing his glasses up his nose.

A heavy feeling pulled Clara's stomach towards the grass. "What?"

"It was Will who was doing the thieving. I know full well where he is – being held in the cellars at the Big House until the police come."

Clara felt like a steamroller was pressing all of the breath from her lungs. "No!"

Robert sighed. "I can't believe it myself. I confessed to Mr Gilbert that I'd let him sleep in the boiler house. I'm not proud of that. To think I brought him here and all he's done is taken advantage of my…kindness."

"No…the soldier who caught him…Thomas. He is the thief," said Clara.

Robert's mouth twisted into a grimace. "It's you and Will who've made a mistake, Clara. Thomas is Mr Gilbert's brother. He was watching the hothouses last night as a favour to Mr and Mrs Gilbert – and me. I've been so tired lately…what with all the extra work in the gardens." Robert's eyes flicked sideways to the hothouses, then back to Clara. He reached up under his glasses and pressed the corner of his cloudy eye, as if trying to clear away the murkiness.

Clara's mind spun like a Catherine wheel nailed to a fence on bonfire night. Thomas was Mr Gilbert's brother. Which meant he was family – Mrs Gilbert's brother-in-law. But why was he so upset when they were in the woods together?

"But it's impossible," Clara said. "Will isn't the thief. We have to help him."

Robert shook his head. "There's nothing I can do for him now. It's in the hands of the police – and the Earl."

"But he's your brother," said Clara, her voice cracking in her throat.

Robert's lips were as thin as a paper cut. "Come on. I need to get you back to the cottage. I've things to do."

Clara's skin tingled. He had things to do? What could be more important than helping his brother? She shook her head. And she carried on shaking it as she pushed past Robert and sprinted across the grass to Gardener's Cottage.

Mr Gilbert was sitting at the bottom of the stairs, his cap in his hands. He stood up as she walked in. "Wherever have you been?" he said, his voice low with disappointment.

Mrs Gilbert came running from the kitchen, her bare feet slapping on the tiles, her nightdress billowing behind her. "Oh, Clara," she said, a hand flying to her neck, fiddling with her necklace. "We've been so worried."

But at that moment Clara did not care if they had

been worried or not. "Will is not the fruit thief!" she said, the words bursting from her lips.

Mr Gilbert's normally ruddy cheeks were an unusual shade of pink. He strode to where Clara was standing. "How do you know about Will?"

Clara straightened her shoulders. "He's my friend."

Mr and Mrs Gilbert exchanged disbelieving looks which tightened their jaws and narrowed their eyes.

"You...know this boy...this thief?" The furrows between Mr Gilbert's eyebrows stood to attention like exclamation marks.

"He would not have taken the fruits. I swear it. He can't have...because...I was with him." She looked at the floor.

Silence peppered the hallway.

Clara glanced up. Anger. Bewilderment. Disbelief. These were some of the emotions that twisted Mr Gilbert's features into a face she did not recognize at all.

"You come with me," Mr Gilbert eventually said in a gruff voice, taking her by the arm. His grip pinched a little. She tried to pull away, but his fingers tightened. "Come with me and I'll show you the damage that boy has done. And then you tell me whether or not he's your friend."

Mr Gilbert's strides were large and purposeful as they made their way across the grass to the hothouses, which winked in the misty early-morning sun. It was something of a mocking wink, as if they knew the truth and were withholding it. Clara desperately tried to piece together everything that had happened, to arrange the facts so that she could convince Mr Gilbert they had made a terrible mistake in apprehending Will.

At the top of the steps, Mr Gilbert paused. "This is the pineapple house," he said, glancing at Clara.

"I know," she replied.

Mr Gilbert stared at her for a second. "You were in here last night? With…Will?"

Clara nodded. Thomas must have told Mr Gilbert he had seen someone with Will. Had the Gilberts checked her bed, found her missing? A small snake of guilt curled around her middle.

Mr Gilbert shook his head, turned abruptly and walked down the steps. "I thought better of you. I really did."

A flush stained Clara's cheeks. She followed Mr Gilbert down the steps, squeezing her hands into fists in her pockets.

Mr Gilbert walked to the middle of a planting row and paused. Clara stood beside him. He was staring at a pineapple plant, at the crown of leaves brushing the soil. It was Will's favourite plant, the Scarlet Brazilian, the one that was just ripe. Except...the pineapple had been hacked off from its stem – it was no longer there. The plant had been cut roughly, without care, leaving a jagged white scar where it had been.

"No," she said breathlessly. "Not the Scarlet Brazilian. Will would not have done this. He loves this plant."

Mr Gilbert gave her a sidelong glance. "This is what your friend did last night, Clara." His tone sent a chill down her back.

"No," Clara said again. Her voice was small, and seemed not to belong to her at all. "We were watching for the thief last night – we've been watching every night."

Mr Gilbert's eyes widened like overfilled balloons. For one awful moment Clara feared they might pop. "That was irresponsible. Not to say dangerous. What would your parents say?"

Clara's skin bristled. "We thought if we caught the thief, you might give Will a job in the gardens. He's good, Mr Gilbert. He knows so much about plants and how they grow. He draws them in his notebook. If you would only look at it—"

"I've seen it," Mr Gilbert interrupted in a grim tone. "There was a list of the produce he's taken. He's spun you a tale, Clara, made you his accomplice."

Clara swelled with frustration. Why did he not understand?

"The fruits were found in the boiler house. In a sack. Pineapples, figs and a handful of peaches," said Mr Gilbert.

In the boiler house? Clara closed her eyes for a second, her insides feeling like a scooped-out eggshell.

"Did Will tell you that Robert is his brother?" Mr Gilbert asked.

Clara flicked her eyes open and nodded.

"Robert says young Will had a bit of a reputation back home, for stealing and the like."

Clara's legs buckled. She stared at Mr Gilbert. She stared at the sorry-looking pineapple stalk. Was this true? Had Will pulled the wool over her eyes – led her to believe he was something he wasn't? She remembered his eyes as he spoke about the fruits…his tears as he buried his father's possessions… Were those the actions of a thief? Her heart was beating fast – too fast. Blood was pounding in her ears. She turned on her heel and ran out of the door.

"Clara. Wait!" cried Mr Gilbert.

His voice bounced from her ears as she ran up the slope, past the orchard and The Bothy and towards the Big House and the one person who could still save Will.

CHAPTER 31

The Hall Boy

Clara walked briskly up the hill, glancing behind her every few minutes, but hers were the only boots treading up the road to the Big House. Mr Gilbert was not following her.

It was near breakfast time, which meant the house staff would be eating together in the servants' hall – an event Mrs Gilbert sometimes spoke about (often reporting tales of sloppily dressed housemaids or footmen who had lost their neckties). Which also meant Clara should have a greater chance of sneaking into the House unnoticed.

She hovered at the steps to the servants' entrance. She straightened her back, picked some fluff from her grey woollen cardigan and tucked her hair behind her ears. Robert seemed determined to have nothing further to do with Will. He said it was in the hands of the police and the Earl – so it was the Earl she needed to persuade to free Will. But before she found the Earl, she would try and find Will himself. She had to talk to him about what had happened the night before, and let him know she hadn't given up on him.

At the bottom of the steps, Clara found herself opening a door which led to a dimly lit corridor filled with a low humming noise, much like a small bee swarm. The noise was coming from a strange box-shaped contraption on the floor filled with coils and wires and metal. A generator for the electric lights. She lowered her head and walked quickly down the corridor, the lights flickering every so often as if protesting about how hard they had to work. She was lucky and had not encountered anyone yet, but she needed to be quick. The passageways were sure to be bustling with activity as soon as breakfast had finished. The ceiling became lower, the corridor narrower, the lights fewer. "Hello, dank, gloomy corridor," Clara whispered under her breath as she passed under a brick archway, and then another. Saying the words calmed her, and made her skipping heart beat a little slower.

A barking cough came from Clara's right.

She jumped back against the wall. There was another cough, the type that would make your ribs ache. It came from a dark recess in the wall between two of the arches.

"Will?" Clara whispered. As her eyes adjusted, she saw that the recess was piled high with coal. On top of the coal perched two owl-like eyes.

"You shouldn't be down here, Miss," the eyes said. They blinked. The eyes were attached to a head. A boy's head, his hair and face almost as dark as the coal pile.

Clara cast an anxious glance up and down the corridor. What if the boy called for help? Would the cook or the butler come running and put a stop to Clara's plan before it began?

"I'm looking for the cellars," Clara said quickly. "Can you help?"

The boy scrabbled down from the top of the coal pile, pieces of coal chasing him like a miniature rockfall.

Clara bent down and picked a piece up, holding it out in her palm.

The boy stepped forward. He was not much older

230

than she was. Underneath the coal dust, his thick hair was rusty-red.

Red. Was this the hall boy Robert and Will had spoken of?

The boy took the coal from Clara's outstretched hand, threw it onto the pile behind him and wiped his hands on his trousers (although as far as Clara could see, that would only serve to make them dirtier still).

"My friend is being held in the cellars. I need to speak with him. It's jolly urgent," Clara said.

The boy's eyes narrowed. He glanced down the corridor, then back at Clara. Did he not know how to talk? He coughed again. His eyes watered. Clara pulled her handkerchief from her pocket and offered it to him.

"Thank you, Miss. But I will stain it."

Clara pushed it into his hand. "Take it. And please, call me Clara. You're Red, aren't you?"

He nodded, staring at the small embroidered daisy on the left-hand corner of the handkerchief. He rubbed his eyes and cheeks, streaking the white cloth with black. Beneath the dust, Red's cheeks were almost translucent, like a creature who lived mostly underground. He offered Clara the dirty handkerchief.

"No. You keep it," she said, giving him a quick smile.

Women's voices drifted down the corridor. They were getting closer. Red scrabbled around for the last pieces of fallen coal and hurled them onto the pile. He gave Clara a quick push, and she suddenly found her stomach pressed against a wall, her back to the coal pile. Red looked at Clara and put a finger to his lips.

Clara felt her right eyelid twitch. Fear wobbled her knees. What would the women do if they caught her lurking in the depths of the Earl's house? Would she be locked in the cellars with Will? An image of her mother's and father's shocked eyes when they heard about her recklessness sprang into her head. She would be able to cope with their crossness, but their disappointment would be hard to bear.

"...I can't stop thinking about that blasted Zeppelin that drifted off course over the Norfolk coast last week," said a woman's voice.

"Scare the living daylights out of me, they do," said another voice.

Clara held her breath. They were so close she could hear them breathing.

"Have you seen the pictures of the bombs? Huge big things, like bells. You'd be flattened if one of those got you."

The voices grew muffled as they walked away.

Clara's heart was beating hard against her ribs.

"It's clear," Red whispered.

Clara crunched over the coal, her boots slipping and sliding.

Red's forehead furrowed. "Oh," he said with dismay.

Clara followed his gaze to the collar of her dress and her cardigan. They were smudged with dust, as if she had rolled in the coal like a dog. As was her apron. As were her hands. "Can you show me where the cellars are?" Clara asked quickly, pushing all thoughts of Mrs Gilbert's reaction to her clothes away.

Red glanced nervously up and down the corridor.

"This is important. My friend Will has been accused of stealing. Please help me, Red. I must talk to him before I speak with the Earl."

Red's eyes widened. He jammed his hands into his pockets and shook his head, pressing his lips together tight.

Clara stared at him. Would Red help her? And if he didn't, what an earth should she do next?

CHAPTER 32

In the Cellars

Clara stared at Red as they lurked in the shadows of the servants' corridors. "No one is allowed to speak to the Earl," Red said to her in shock. "Except his butler. And the housekeeper. Maybe some other people too. But not the likes of us."

"But I have to," said Clara. "Before the police come to take Will away. Only the Earl can help."

Red chewed on his lip. "You're a good friend to this…Will," he said, a little enviously, Clara thought.

"I'm trying to be," Clara replied.

Red pulled Clara's handkerchief from his pocket and blew his nose. "Your friend Will – is he Robert's brother – the gardener with the funny eye? Has he been staying in the boiler house in the gardens?"

Clara nodded.

"Robert owes me some coins for keeping quiet about that," Red said, scrunching Clara's handkerchief into a ball.

"He hasn't paid you?" Clara asked.

Red shook his head and lowered his eyes. "The coins aren't for me. Pa's away fighting and there are six of us to feed at home."

"I have some money," Clara said. This was perhaps an even bigger emergency than the broken tapestry. She just hoped her parents agreed when she next saw them.

Red looked up and smiled. He glanced down the passage again. "Soon the corridors will be filled with people leaving breakfast. We'll need to be quick." Red was whippet-fast as he led Clara along the winding corridor, ducking past the kitchens where the smell of warm bread and frying bacon made Clara's stomach groan and gurgle. They passed another staircase leading upwards. "You'll find the Earl up there, most likely in the library this time of day – reading the early papers. It's at the back of the entrance hall."

"Thank you," said Clara, giving him a broad smile.

The blush which stole onto Red's cheeks shone through the streaks of coal dust.

The corridor began to narrow and Red paused in front of a small open doorway leading to a winding spiral staircase. "Cellars are down there," he whispered, his eyes darting back and forth. "I'll stay here and keep watch."

Dampness curled around Clara's neck, sending a clammy tremor down her back. The electric wall lights were dimmer in the stairwell than in the corridor, the flickering more frequent.

A cough rasped up the stone stairs.

Red's eyes widened.

Clara's heart almost stopped in her chest. *Will.* She ran lightly down the twisting staircase until she arrived in the cellar. It smelled musty and damp. One electric light buzzed and hummed, the far corners of the cellar hidden in the dark. Iron gates – prison-like gates – filled the gaps between three arches, behind which lay half-empty wine racks, wooden boxes and dusty barrels. The gates to each archway were shut – and padlocked.

Clara stood for a second, letting her eyes adjust to the darkness. She had no urge to greet this horrible place. The only thing she wanted to do was find her friend. "Will," she whispered. "Are you there?"

There was a scuffling behind the metal bars of the middle archway. Then another cough, which made Clara's toes curl in her boots. Will's pale-as-the-moon face appeared from the gloom. His fingers clutched the metal bars. They rattled, sending an echo bouncing around the cellar. "Clara?" he said, his voice loaded with disbelief.

"I can't believe they've locked you up down here," Clara cried. Her feet felt heavy as she ran to him.

"It wasn't me," Will said in a cracked voice. "I didn't take the fruits. I swear it." He slumped to the floor, wrapping his arms around his knees. "I was wrong, Clara. I wanted to believe it was Mrs Gilbert taking the fruits. But it wasn't."

Clara swallowed, kneeled in front of Will and gripped the metal bars. "It wasn't Thomas either, Will. He is Mr Gilbert's brother."

"I know. Thomas said after he'd caught me," Will said miserably.

Clara held onto the bars a little tighter. "Robert said...you have stolen things before."

Will lurched forward. "I didn't, Clara. I swear on my father's life."

"But why would your brother say such things?"

Clara whispered. "And why were the stolen pineapples hidden in the boiler house? Who put them there?"

Will's face crumpled. He wiped his nose on the back of his hand. "Robert…he got in trouble. When he was younger."

Clara's insides unfurled. "What?" The metal bars felt cool against her palms.

"He stole from a neighbour. It was a joke gone wrong. There was a fight and Robert got hit in the eye… almost lost his sight. When Father found out, I'd never seen him so angry. That's when Robert left home and got the job here on the estate. Father tried to make things right when we came to visit. But…it was never the same between them. When we left, Robert said he wanted nothing more to do with Father, that he never wanted to see him again. He never did."

Clara sat back on her heels. Robert's eye had been injured in a fight? He had lied to her – he'd said he was born with his eye like that. His argument with their father – was that why he had been so quick to deny he had any family, and refused to come with Will to bury their father's things? Was that why he had said on their trip to the hospital that some disappointments would stay with you for ever?

Will's eyes were grey pools of pain. Clara wished with all her might that she could make herself small, slink through the bars and comfort her friend until his face was less broken and more Will-like again.

"I'm sorry. I should have been honest with you from the start. But Robert's all I have left. If he goes to prison…" Will whispered.

Like the strike of a match, the thought came to Clara in an instant. "All this time…you thought *Robert* was the one stealing the fruits?" she said softly.

Will nodded. "I'm sorry I accused your aunt. I half-believed it might be her, after you'd told me about seeing her with the basket, and then seeing her with Thomas in the woods. But deep down…I knew it was my brother."

Clara was shocked. She had been diverted by Will and Mrs Gilbert and Thomas and had not given Robert a second thought. Clara had trusted Robert, liked him. But what kind of person let their younger brother take the blame for something they had done? "You think he put the fruits in the boiler house to make it seem like you stole them?"

"He had a key. He could have come in any time he liked," Will said, wiping his nose on the back of his hand.

"Do you think he knew we were trying to catch the thief?" Clara asked.

Will nodded. "And used it to his advantage. He would have known Mr Gilbert's brother was going to keep watch in the hothouse – and that he'd catch us in there. Robert could have taken the fruit afterwards and hidden it in the boiler house. But don't hate him for it. There will be a reason he has done it."

A reason? But if Will was right, Robert had stolen from the Earl and may have planned that Will would take the blame all along. "Are you sure about this, Will? Your own brother…"

Will dropped his head into his hands. "I'm not sure of anything any more, Clara. I have no proof it was him. If I'd asked him, he would have just denied it. I thought if we kept watch…it would put him off…be a warning. I didn't want him to get into trouble."

"I will go and tell the Earl…he will free you—" Clara said firmly.

"The Earl? What good will that do?" Will interrupted, his voice tight. "No one will believe it's Robert."

"I believe it was Robert. I know you would never steal those pineapples." Clara reached through the bars, grabbed one of Will's hands and pushed all of her warmth and hope and bravery into his palm. She would get him out of these cellars. She just hoped the Earl would listen.

CHAPTER 33

The Big House

As Red led Clara to the servants' staircase to the main part of the Big House, she wondered how she should address the Earl. Should she drop into a curtsey, or shake his hand? She uncurled her fists and groaned inwardly at the sight of her coal-stained fingers and the dirt under her nails. She looked as if she belonged in a coal pit. She wiped them on her apron but that just added to the existing filth. At the foot of the stairs, bright lights shone down from the Big House, beckoning her upwards. A blackboard was attached to the wall. Clara's breath caught in her throat as she read the cursive chalk writing.

<u>*Message from the housekeeper*</u>

*Servants rules to be observed when entering
the upstairs areas of the house*

*Ensure your voice is <u>never</u> heard by the ladies
and gentlemen of the house*

*Always make room and turn away if you
meet one of your employers*

*<u>Never</u> offer your opinion to the ladies and
gentlemen of the house*

*Unless your duties require it, <u>do not</u> touch
the furniture or belongings of any of the ladies
and gentlemen of the house*

*Any breakages or damages to the house will
be deducted from wages*

Signed: Mrs Gilbert

Voices. Getting nearer. Clara's feet froze to the stone floor.

"Go, Clara. Now."

She turned.

Red gave her a desperate glance. "I will divert them," he said. He darted off in the direction of the voices.

The footsteps paused. "You are not supposed to be in this corridor," a woman's voice said sternly.

"I...kn-know..." stammered Red.

His voice spurred Clara's feet forward. She ran up the stairs, past the words on the blackboard, which seemed to be giving her a disapproving stare. She paused in front of the door which led into the gentlemen's part of the Big House – to the Earl and his family. She cracked it open and could see a grand entrance hall with glossy berry-red marble pillars, which stretched to a high ceiling capped by a glass dome. Gilded paintings as large as she was hung on the walls, and in the centre of the hallway was a plinth bearing a white marble carving of an enormous pineapple.

The fear knotting Clara's stomach tightened as she opened the door fully and stepped into the hallway. Although this was too huge and sumptuous to be called a hallway. Her hallway at home could fit into this one a hundred times over. Clara blinked. She wished she could stand for a while, saying hello to each and every painting, statue and wall hanging. The black-and-white marbled floor. The shiny wooden tables adorned with china ornaments. The display of flowers which scented the air with the smells of summer. But there was no time for any of that. She had to find the library, and fast. She took a step onto the marble. *Click-click-click.* The noise from her boots echoed around the cavernous room. Bending down, she quickly slipped off her boots and, clutching them in her right hand, half-ran, half-slid across the floor to a large wooden door at the back of the hall. It was at least three times the height she was – fit for a giant.

She heard a murmur from inside. Was that the Earl?

"Hey, you there." The voice came from behind her. She turned. There was a man, smartly dressed in a black tailcoat, with a white shirt and gloves – a butler. "Who are you? What in heaven's name are you doing up here?"

Clara turned back to the door, grasped the huge bronze doorknob and gave it a twist. It didn't move.

The butler was approaching, his footsteps echoing.

She gave the door a push. A larger push.

"Wait. You can't go in there. Stop!"

Clara threw all of her weight against the door, which swung open with a low groan, tipping her into the room. She gasped. Pineapple-yellow marble pillars. Silky green sofas and easy chairs. A large crystal chandelier twinkled in the sun streaming in through the floor-to-ceiling windows. Masses and masses of bookshelves. A fire crackled in the grate, the chimney so huge that Clara and her entire family could stand inside it with room to spare.

Clara heard another murmur, saw the back of a narrow head, with thin hair that was greying at the nape of the neck. A trail of pipe-smoke puffed to the ceiling.

As she took a step forward she felt a hand clamp on her shoulder.

"That's far enough, Missy," the butler said under his breath.

Clara tried to twist from his grasp, but his fingers were holding her tight.

The greying head was turning, as the man rose from the chair, his pipe in his hand. The newspaper he had been holding dropped to the rug.

"I say, what on earth is going on, Richardson?"

"I am so sorry, Sir. I am not sure how she got in," the butler said in a clipped voice. His nails dug into Clara's skin and she squirmed.

The Earl's eyes narrowed. He looked Clara up and down. At the boots still clutched in her hand. At the streaks of coal dust on her apron and her face.

The hothouses. Will. Robert. The stolen pineapples.

Everything Clara wanted to say jumbled and spun in her head.

The butler steered her to the door. "I am so sorry, Sir. I will get rid of her immediately."

No. This wasn't how it was supposed to be. As the butler steered her away from the Earl, Clara's fingers unclenched, and her boots thudded onto the shiny parquet floor. She grabbed onto a small console table as she was pushed to the door. A small china figurine of a shepherd boy standing next to a woolly sheep wobbled. Clara held her breath as it rolled to the edge of the table. She lurched forward, tried to save it, but she wasn't quick enough. The china boy fell, his angelic head separating from his body with a loud crack and rolling under the table. She looked at the pieces of (no doubt precious) china with a large helping of dismay. Another lovely thing broken – but unlike Mrs Gilbert's tapestry frame, she very much doubted she had enough coins remaining in her purse to replace it. The Earl would be furious and surely wouldn't want to hear what she had to say about Will. And if that was the case, how was she to help her friend now?

CHAPTER 34

The Earl

The tick-tock of the grandfather clock in the corner. The crackle of the fire in the grate. The sharp intake of breath from the butler. Clara's ears burned. "Oh," she said, dropping to her knees. She scooped the broken pieces of china into her hands. "Oh dear."

"Give that here," said the butler through gritted teeth. "You will be charged with trespassing and damage to private property. Shall I inform the police, Sir?"

Clara sat back on her heels, staring at the broken china. She thought about the rules Mrs Gilbert had written on the blackboard. She was about to break one more. She stood up and stared into the Earl's furrowed face. "I'm sorry for the breakage...Sir. But I came to speak with you because you need to know that the boy being held in the cellars – he is not the pineapple thief."

The butler grabbed her shoulder again with an even tighter grip. "I knew it. Friendly with that other trespasser, she is."

"Wait." The Earl held up his palm. He laid his pipe down next to a glass bowl containing a few mandarins, picked up his newspaper and folded it, all the while looking at Clara. "Perhaps it's best if we start with introductions. And you are?"

"Clara. Mrs Gilbert's niece," she said, her voice wavering.

"Mrs Gilbert's niece. *Our* Mrs Gilbert. The housekeeper?"

Clara nodded. Perhaps Mrs Gilbert didn't undertake her work as invisibly as she thought.

The Earl gave his butler a firm nod. "That will be all, Richardson."

Richardson's clawlike hand dropped from Clara's shoulder. "But, Sir…"

"I said that will be all." The Earl gave his butler a stony look. Clara could almost hear the butler's skin prickling and cracking in indignation. He left the room and gently closed the door.

The Earl beckoned Clara forward.

Clara held the broken figurine in her open palm. "I am sorry…I will ask my parents to loan me the money to pay for a new one."

The Earl gave her a small smile. "That was a wedding present from a distant cousin in France. Never liked the blessed thing." But there was something wistful in the Earl's voice which made Clara wonder if he was telling the whole truth. He took the broken pieces from her and carefully laid them next to the bowl of mandarins.

"Please let Will go. He is not a thief," Clara said quietly.

The Earl's eyes narrowed.

"He…loves the gardens. It is his ambition to work there one day. He loves the pineapples like…family. Except, now he has no family. If he is charged with stealing it will ruin him. He will surely go to prison."

The Earl turned to the fire, which was spitting in the grate.

"I have spoken with the boy's brother – a gardener. Robert, isn't it? It seems this Will has rather a reputation for stealing."

"No. You are wrong."

The Earl rubbed his right ear, as if those were unusual words for him to hear.

Will was in those dank cellars, depending on her to make things right. "It is the other way around. It is Robert who took the fruits."

The Earl turned to look at her, his head tilted. "That is…rather a serious accusation." He rubbed his chin. "Do you have any evidence?"

Clara stared at him blankly. Evidence. She had no evidence at all.

"Do you like books, Clara?"

Clara nodded.

"What are you reading right now?" the Earl asked.

Clara blinked. The conversation had taken a rather curious turn. "*The Jungle Book*," she said.

"Ah, yes. Mr Kipling does spin a good adventurous tale, doesn't he?" The Earl's eyes flickered to the bookshelves. "I am very partial to the odd detective story, myself. Sherlock Holmes is a particular favourite. If I were him, I would be saying to you that the evidence presented to me is irrefutable. I have seen with my own eyes the sack of fruit found in the boiler house, the list of stolen fruit in the boy's notebook. And his drawings of the hothouses and the pineapples. Although I must say, they really were rather good." The Earl scratched his chin, gave Clara a long searching look and waited for her to speak.

But she had nothing to say. Nothing at all. Clara felt like a sailing boat, at sea with no wind. The Earl was right. She had no proof that Robert had taken the pineapples. There was nothing she could do or say to save Will.

The Earl rang a small silver bell. Richardson appeared and gave a small bow. He appeared to be breathless, as if he had been running up flights of stairs.

"See that Miss Clara returns safely to Gardener's Cottage," the Earl said.

Richardson nodded and gave Clara an imperious look. "It is already arranged, Sir. I sent a message down to Mrs Gilbert. She is on her way to collect the girl."

Clara saw the glimmer in Richardson's eyes. It implied he knew full well what a telling-off Clara was going to get from her aunt when she arrived. Clara pushed her hands into the pockets of her apron and straightened her shoulders. She would take all the punishments thrown at her in order to try and clear Will's name, but it was clear she was fast running out of time.

CHAPTER 35

A Stormy Night

Mrs Gilbert did not utter a single word to Clara as they walked down the hill to Gardener's Cottage. Her hair was pulled into a severe bun. It exposed the pale skin near her eyes, the faint unused laughter lines, like rusty spokes on a bicycle wheel. When Richardson had handed Clara over, Mrs Gilbert had given him a curt nod. Richardson had given her a haughty stare in return, which had caused Mrs Gilbert to sniff, pull Clara's arm and steer her away from the House.

As they passed the stable block, Clara saw Robert cleaning out the horse cart, stacking it with empty crates ready to be loaded with produce for the hospital. He lifted his head as they walked past. Clara lowered hers, biting the inside of her lip until it was sore. How could he let Will take the blame for something he had done? Anger rose inside her like a storm.

Mr Gilbert was waiting on the front step as they walked up the gravel path. He stepped to one side, letting Mrs Gilbert and Clara pass through the door. He puffed out a mountainous sigh. It made Clara feel ever so slightly sick.

Mrs Gilbert led Clara into the parlour, then stood with her back to the window and fiddled with the cross she wore around her neck, rubbing her thumb over the gold. So much had happened and it was still only a little after 10 o'clock. Mr Gilbert had lit a small fire. Clara had never seen the flames shiver to life in the morning before. Perhaps it meant she would be spending quite some time in this room with her aunt and uncle, discussing her wrongdoings.

"So," Mr Gilbert said in a low voice, coming to stand beside his wife. "You ran away from me and took it upon yourself to visit the Earl. This will not do, Clara. It's not how things work around here."

Clara thought of Mrs Gilbert's rules chalked onto the blackboard. She had broken all of them in a single hour. "I just wanted to help Will."

"Thomas caught Will. The boy cannot be helped," Mr Gilbert said.

Clara's skin tightened. She glanced beyond Mrs Gilbert, out of the window to the small lake. Two swans were gliding across the water, their necks like question marks. "Why did you meet Thomas in the early morning, give him produce from the gardens and comfort him when he cried, Mrs Gilbert?" she asked in a rush. "Why did you write those letters – the ones in the locked room upstairs?"

Mrs Gilbert's face was almost transparent, like all the blood had leeched from it. "Frank," she whispered.

Mr Gilbert's cheeks flushed pink.

Clara's eyes flicked from her aunt to her uncle and back again.

"You've been in Frank's room? Read my letters to him?" Mrs Gilbert's voice was shrill.

"Frank's room?" Clara asked in confusion.

"He was six. Only six," Mrs Gilbert said. Her eyes were wild and bright.

Clara shrank away from the Gilberts, until heat from the fire flared against the backs of her legs.

"Frank was our nephew," Mr Gilbert said. "My brother's child – Thomas's son. He came to stay with us two summers ago. There was an accident. Frank…died. I've found it…hard to speak to my brother Thomas since it happened. The guilt, you see." He looked at the ceiling. "When Lizzy found out that Thomas was camping on the estate with the Regiment, she decided to talk to him, to try and mend things between us."

Clara nibbled on a thumbnail. The talk in Mrs Gilbert's letters of picnics and Kitty the horse. These were all things a child had done. The person in her letters was a boy.

Mrs Gilbert sank to her knees on the rug like a deflated balloon. Mr Gilbert kneeled beside her, placed an arm around her shoulders and stroked a stray hair from her cheek. It was so tender it made Clara's throat ache. Mrs Gilbert pulled away from her husband's arm, wiping her nose on a handkerchief. "We did not have children of our own and Frank was like a son to me that summer. I suppose that those letters are my way of dealing with…the grief. When I write, it's almost as if he's still with us." Her bottom lip wobbled.

"I'm sorry. Father never told me," Clara said quietly.

Mrs Gilbert glanced up. "Some things are too difficult to say." She turned her head to the window. "Frank loved the hothouses, especially when it was stormy. We would pretend we were in a ship at sea, the rain and wind howling and rattling the glass." She swallowed. "One evening, he begged me to take him to the pineapple house. He loved it there the most – the warm earthy smell, the plants. Little heads, he called them. He would speak to them, give them names. Maestro was his favourite."

Maestro. The name on the piece of paper under the tapestry. The inscription on the brass plate, *Deep peace of the quiet earth* – that was in memory of little Frank.

"The wind was fierce as we ran across the gardens. It happened in an instant. A branch fell from the tree near the hothouses. The Earl knew it was too close to the pineapple house. He'd been talking about removing it as it had grown so big, but no decision had been made. His daughters liked to play in that tree, you see, and there was no sign it was unsafe. The branch hit us both – me on the leg and Frank on the head." Mrs Gilbert rubbed her neck. "He died instantly. He did not suffer."

Tears burned Clara's throat.

"The Earl…was devastated. He sometimes leaves fruits on the tree stump by the pineapple house and in other places in the gardens where Frank liked to play – his way of remembering, I suppose."

The mandarins she and Will had found – they had not been connected to the fruit thief at all. The Earl had left them because he felt so terrible about Frank's death.

"The Earl is generous and allows us to help ourselves to produce from the gardens. I've been passing the extra vegetables to Thomas for the Regiment, trying to do some good," Mrs Gilbert said. "Mr Gilbert and Robert were worn out with the worry of the stolen fruits, so Thomas offered to help – to watch the hothouses."

"I'm glad he did," said Mr Gilbert. He gave his wife a small smile, as if perhaps things between him and his brother could be mended after all.

Clara cleared her throat. "I didn't mean to pry…or go through your things, Mrs Gilbert. And I'm truly sorry about Frank. It's just…Mother had written to you and not me. And I thought you were…hiding things."

Mrs Gilbert reached up and grasped Clara's right hand, giving it a squeeze. She pulled her down to the rug, until they were sitting opposite each other. Mrs Gilbert's fingers were icy, like they had been dipped in a frozen pond. "I'm sorry I treated you so badly…you just…reminded me of what I had lost. The responsibility of having another child staying here…I found it hard.

And you should call me Aunt Elizabeth. It…will be nice to hear that name again." Her aunt's hands felt less icy now, her face a little less pale and broken. "And I did hear from your mother, Clara. But she did not write. I spoke to her on the telephone – at the Big House."

Her mother had not written? She had been searching for letters which did not exist?

"She…did not want to write until things were more…certain," Clara's uncle said gruffly.

Her aunt's face flushed a rosy pink. "We have been keeping a secret from you, Clara," she said in a whisper. "About your family."

Clara's insides folded in on themselves like a concertina.

Her aunt stared straight into Clara's eyes. "But I think it's time you knew the truth."

Chapter 36

Clara's Envelope

The truth, the truth, the truth. The words rolled around Clara's head in time with her breaths, which were jerky, like she had been skipping or jumping. She quickly pulled from her pocket the crumpled letter from the War Office and held it out to her aunt.

Her aunt's forehead crinkled. "What's this?"

"I…took it from the post-boy, just before Mother and Father left for Devon. I didn't mean to keep it…but Father was so ill, and I was so worried. Then they left, and it was too late. I was going to give it to you, but then you…" Clara paused.

Clara's aunt gave her a look filled with quiet

understanding. "I suppose I wasn't quite the person you thought I was."

Clara gave her a brief nod.

"Open the letter," said Clara's aunt, as she stared at the War Office stamp. Her lips were quivering. Was that because she imagined the same terrible news as Clara? She thought of Will, and how he had told her there was nothing worse than not knowing the truth. She thought of how Father had told her to be brave. She *had* been brave. She had found Will in the cellars, and confronted the Earl. Despite all this, Clara's hands still shook as she slid a finger into the back of the envelope and slit it open. She pulled the single sheet of paper out. The typeface was blurry and swam in front of her eyes like tadpoles in a pool.

```
...Private Christopher Millar has been
transferred to the Red Cross auxiliary
hospital in Plymouth...cautiously optimistic
that with extensive rehabilitation he will
make a full recovery...
```

Clara blinked. Christopher wasn't fatally wounded? He would recover?

Clara's aunt prised the letter from her fingers. "We were so sorry to hear that your brother was injured."

Clara blinked again. "You knew?"

Her aunt nodded. "The War Office sent an earlier telegram to your parents. It wasn't as optimistic as this, and it asked them to come to Devon immediately. There had been a mix-up at the casualty clearing station in Rouen. Christopher was taken to Plymouth, rather than back to your home in Kent."

"So…Father did not go to Devon to convalesce?" Clara said slowly. Everything she thought had been true was being undone in her head.

"No," said Clara's aunt. "Although I think the sea air has done him the world of good. Your mother says his lungs are finally improving. You will be able to go home in a few days."

Will had been right. If she had been able to face her fears earlier and open the letter, she would not have wasted all this time worrying and wondering.

Aunt Elizabeth reached across and placed a hand on Clara's knee. "Your mother said you took it very badly when your father had gas poisoning. That it gave you terrible nightmares. They thought it best you stay with us until the news was more…certain."

Nightmares. But those had been because of her father's stories. Or had they? Father had started telling her the bedtime stories when he had returned from France, on the nights neither of them could sleep. Had he been telling her about mountain-crossing fearless explorers to make her feel braver, more able to deal with the war and all of its terribleness? She sucked in a breath and let these new thoughts settle until they felt more at home in her head.

But even though most of the mysteries had been solved, the biggest one remained.

"But what about Will and the thefts?" Clara asked quietly.

Her uncle shook his head. "I'll hear no more talk of this now. We have proof that Will stole the fruit, Clara. I'm afraid that's all there is to it. The police will shortly be arriving to take him into town. They will charge him with theft. I'm afraid things are looking very bad for that boy indeed."

It was early evening, the sky a quiet shade of damson. Leaves from the apple and pear trees coated the grass in a crisp, russet carpet. A cacophony of birds chirped a

263

soulful tune, saying goodbye to another day. Clara sat with her back to a tree trunk, closed her eyes and thought of Will. She had felt his sorrow when burying his father's things; the joy in his eyes when he was with the pineapples; the delight and care he took in his drawings and his hope for a better life. There had to be a way of stopping the police from charging him, for she knew deep in her bones that he truly was innocent. She needed to be a detective like the Earl had said, and find some firm evidence that proved Robert was the thief.

Something small and light plopped onto her apron. A little green caterpillar. It wriggled on its back, its legs waving feebly in the air. Clara gently rolled it over and held out a finger. "Hello, you," she said. The caterpillar cautiously clambered aboard and inched towards her wrist.

Clara heard the front door of The Bothy open. Robert came out and sat on the front step. He leaned against the brick wall, tipped his head back and closed his eyes. His hands gripped his knees tightly. He had seemed so nice when she had first arrived, with his talk of visiting faraway places where the pineapples were grown. She had thought he had been protecting Will by hiding him in the boiler house, when instead his intentions had been cruel. Anger curled under her skin.

The caterpillar's feet tickled Clara's arm. It would be finding a place to build its chrysalis soon, to turn into something else entirely and fly away. Clara blinked. Something clicked in her head, like a key being turned. Her thoughts gathered speed, pieces of the puzzle clicking into place.

The Bothy was quiet, the gardeners up at the Big House having tea. Will had said Robert shared a room on the ground floor with some of the other under-gardeners, and this was where she found herself. She crept along the hall, pulled on a door latch and peered inside. Three beds, with a small table next to each. A deep sickness welled in the pit of her stomach. If she was right, this would change everything for Will – and for Robert.

She walked swiftly to the first table. On top lay a gardening manual, a notebook and a pencil. It was the same style of notebook Will had – blue with a bound edge. She flicked through it. The book belonged to a man called George and contained lists of gardening jobs.

She turned to the next table. The top of this one was

clear. She opened the small drawer beneath it and felt around inside. It was empty. She frowned. Whoever slept in that bed had no personal possessions. Unless they did, but they wanted to hide them. Clara turned to the bed and lifted the corner of the mattress. The bed frame creaked loudly. She paused and glanced at the door. The hallway was still quiet.

There was nothing under the bed. She thought of the seam of her own mattress, which had come undone so readily when she had looked for a secret hiding place. She bent down and smoothed her hand around the outside. Nothing.

Frustration billowed through her. It had to be in here somewhere. She cast her eyes around the room. There, on the back of the door – Robert's gardening jacket with its distinctive mustard yellow lining. Hanging in plain sight.

Clara took it down from the hook and felt inside the pockets. They were empty. She patted the jacket down. There was a rustle. Something was hidden in the lining. She reached into the right pocket again and turned it inside out. There was a small hole which had been roughly sewn up, as if it had been mended and undone several times. Clara's jaw tightened.

She pulled the stitching apart and gingerly felt inside. *Papers.* She gave them a tug and they slipped out. She turned the papers over in her hand, the meaning of them slowly dawning on her. She remembered what the Earl had said. This was good evidence, but it wasn't enough. She needed more. She glanced out of the window. The sky was darkening – the gardeners would be returning from the Big House soon. A plan was bubbling; a way to catch Robert and make him confess to his crimes. She just hoped it would work out, for Will's future depended on it.

CHAPTER 37

Courage

Clara watched the bats swooping in the early-evening dark as she approached the stables. The days and nights were cooling as October marched towards the chill of winter. The bats would be hibernating soon, tucking themselves away from the cold in barns and attics. Like the bats, Clara knew her time at Gardener's Cottage was speeding towards an end, and to a new beginning of sorts, back home with her family and friends. But she could not and would not go until she had done everything in her power to help Will. He had no one else in the world to look out for him now – no mother or father to welcome him home at the end of the day, no brother to rely on when times were tough, no bed of his own to sleep in at night.

Robert's papers burned a hole in her pocket as she pulled on the stable door. The cart loaded with vegetables was locked inside. Somehow, this wasn't very surprising. She saw a figure approaching.

"Clara," Robert said in surprise. "What are you doing here?"

Clara summoned all her courage; she imagined drawing it up from a well, buckets and buckets of it. She pulled her shoulders back. "Mr Gilbert asked me to go with you tonight to take the vegetables to the hospital."

Robert frowned. "Really? But he told me to take them tomorrow."

"There's an emergency – a food shortage," Clara said lightly.

Robert's brow furrowed.

"I overheard him telling Mrs Gilbert what a hard worker you are. You're his favourite of all the under-gardeners. I think he may even pay you a little extra this week."

Robert's good eye was as shiny as a spoon. "Really?"

Clara nodded, trying to quell her rising nausea at telling such a lie.

Clara had not been along the country lanes at night before. Robert steered the horse deftly through the dark, like he had done this journey many times. Clara wondered exactly how many times, as she buried her hands under the rug covering their knees. Rage tingled in the tips of her fingers. The rage translated into words she could not keep from rising in her throat. "Have you seen Will?" she asked.

Kitty's hooves clip-clopped on the road. The wind whistled around their heads, flicking strands of Clara's hair into her eyes.

"No," Robert said in a curt voice. "He's been taken into town, to the police station."

Clara thought of her own brother – how terrified she had been of him being injured, how she had been powerless to support him and couldn't bear to think of him at all for a long time. "You should help your brother. He needs you."

"Things are…complicated," Robert said in a thin voice, as the sequin-like lights of the town pushed through the inky blackness.

"Why?" Clara persisted. But Robert did not respond, just stared straight ahead. More words fizzed in her throat – accusing words. She squashed them down. She must not confront Robert yet, not until she had firm proof that he had been taking the fruit.

Smoke curled from the chimneys of the hospital into the dark. A man and a lady walked past with a small dog, out for an early-evening stroll. The dog barked as Robert drew back on the reins and brought Kitty to a slow stop.

Clara hopped down from the cart and stroked Kitty's flank. She was warm, breath steaming from her nose. She nodded her head, as if glad to have arrived. Clara tied Kitty to a lamp post and helped Robert unload the wooden crates of vegetables, stacking them on the roadside. As Robert disappeared through the hospital entrance carrying two of the crates, Clara lifted the corner of a cloth covering a crate still in the back of the cart. Potatoes and carrots. In another were tightly packed beetroot and leeks. Her fingers moved quickly and lightly across the crates, lifting the cloths and making a mental note of the contents. There were no pineapples. No figs or peaches. Clara sighed, picked up one of the smaller crates and walked to the hospital entrance. Maybe she had been wrong after all.

A nurse in a white uniform came through the door

just as Clara was wondering how to open it and hold the crate at the same time. She gave Clara a bright smile. "Food delivery?"

Clara nodded and rushed past her down the corridor, the smell of disinfectant sticking in her throat. Robert walked past her in the opposite direction, two empty crates from the previous delivery in his arms. He gave her a quick nod.

In the kitchen stores a lady was unloading the boxes Robert had delivered. "Is this the last of them?" she asked.

"I think there are a few more," said Clara, putting her crate down. Where was Robert? She listened for the echo of his heavy boots in the corridor, but it was quiet.

Clara half-ran back to the hospital entrance. She flung open the doors and stood on the pavement. Kitty was still standing contentedly, her nose in a bag of hay. Her tail flicked. The last of the boxes were standing on the pavement, waiting to be brought inside. Where had Robert gone?

Clara peered down the street to her left – empty. She swung to the right – also empty. Standing quietly, she let the sounds and sights of the town settling down for the night fill up her senses. The clunk of a window being shut, and the swish of curtains being pulled. A drifting smell of something sweet, like milky cocoa. A mother standing in an open doorway, a swaddled but fretful baby wriggling in her arms. Then...to her right, on the opposite side of the road in the shadows, she noticed a figure. Clara peered into the darkness. Could it be him? She began to run down the long street, her feet light and quiet on the paving slabs. The figure sank into the gloom and reappeared under a pool of light from a street lamp. His head was bent forwards and he was carrying a parcel. *Robert!*

Clara crossed the street and picked up her pace, her eyes never leaving his back. Where was he going?

Boom. The noise was like a loud thunderclap.

Clara pressed on. A sudden storm was the last thing she needed – if the pavements were slick with rain and the air misty, she might lose sight of Robert altogether.

Boom. Boom. Boom. The glass in the windows of the terraced house Clara was passing rattled and shook.

Her feet came to a sudden halt. A strange mechanical whirring noise was coming from the sky. A couple of front doors opened, pale faces peering out into the night. *How very odd*, Clara thought, as the people clapped hands to their mouths (which were open so wide it was a wonder their faces didn't crack apart).

There came the sound of slapping feet on the pavement running towards her.

"Zeppelin," a boy said in a shrill voice as his blurry body ran past. "Zeppelin attack! Take shelter."

Doors were opening. People were leaving their houses, running down the street towards the hospital, in the direction Clara had come from. A father carried a small girl in a nightdress, whose head was tipped towards the sky. "I see it, Papa. It's there, look!"

Clara slowly looked up, in the direction of the noisy whirring. A long, silver cigar-shaped balloon loomed in the sky ahead.

The hair at the nape of her neck lifted and she swallowed a scream, her feet rooted to the spot.

CHAPTER 38

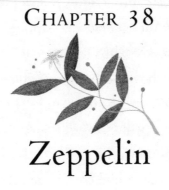

Zeppelin

Clara's heart squashed in her chest. But...they were in Suffolk. Zeppelins didn't come this far north. The threat was in London, in the big cities. Not in small towns in the east of England. Then she remembered what she had overheard at the Big House – how a Zeppelin had drifted in from the Norfolk coast – and the report Mr Gilbert had read in the newspaper. Her hands felt clammy and her stomach churned.

A man pushing a cart jolted into Clara as she stood frozen on the pavement. A small dog and a squawking parrot in a cage were jostled from side to side as he ran. People were taking their precious things and fleeing for their lives. She must follow them – now. Her limbs began to unfreeze into a strange shakiness that made her teeth chatter in her skull.

Clara heard the ringing of a fire bell from behind her and the rumble of the cartwheels on the road. The bell unfroze her brain. *Robert*. His eyes were fixed to the sky as hers had been, but he wasn't standing still, he was running straight into the path of the huge German flying machine.

"Robert!" she yelled. Her voice was small, eaten up by the clamour of the fire bell, the sound of panicked voices and crying children. Why had he not turned back? Did she have enough time to run after him and grab him? Forcing herself forwards, Clara began to pelt down the pavement towards him.

Robert took a right turn, into a narrow cobbled street.

The Zeppelin rumbled overhead.

"Robert!" Clara shouted again. Her voice was croaky, whipped away by the wind. He was knocking on a red door. The parcel he had been carrying was at his feet. He launched himself at the door with both hands, hammering and banging.

"Robert," Clara yelled again.

He turned, his surprised eyes meeting hers.

"The Zeppelin – we need to get out of here, now!" She glanced again at the Zeppelin, which was closer now, turning the gaps of sky between the buildings into a hypnotic and shimmery silver. She dragged her eyes away, back towards Robert. Clara stepped towards him, held out a trembling hand and gestured for him to come with her. "I know what you did. I know you stole the fruits. But it will be okay. We can go and tell Mr Gilbert and…"

Robert glanced at the parcel at his feet. He opened his mouth to speak, but the words did not have time to arrive.

The whistling noise made Clara's ears pop. The orange flash made stars dance in front of her eyes.

Boom.

Time seemed to pause, as if the world was a clock whose hands had been stopped. Clara was flung backwards; her outstretched arm whipped into her side with a heavy thump as she landed on the ground. Everything was spinning, and she did not know which way was up and which was down. A sharp spiral of pain wound along her right leg. Light flickered at the edges of her vision. *Smoke. Fire.*

Everything was on fire. Thick dark smoke choked Clara's lungs and stung her eyes. The pain in her calf worsened. She reached down, felt her ripped stocking. Her fingers came away sticky and warm. *Blood*. She pushed herself upright, the pain making her dizzy. She blinked and coughed, stared at the pile of smoking, dusty rubble where Robert had been standing a few moments before. A piece of red wood lay near her right leg. She suddenly felt as if she was floating above the streets and into the clouds with the Zeppelin. It was the door Robert had been knocking on. It had been splintered into sections, the wood scattered like matchsticks. Which meant Robert…

Clara dragged in a breath of dust, gritted her teeth and rolled onto her knees. She had to find him, for Will's sake. Whatever he had done, Robert was the only family Will had left.

She crawled towards the rubble. "Robert," she croaked.

"Miss? Miss?" Wavering torches. Hands on her shoulders, helping her to her feet.

"No," she said, shrugging them off, wincing at a new burst of pain. "Robert," she croaked again. "There was a man, standing at the door."

"Which door, Miss?" shouted a man, bending over so his ear was close to her mouth. She felt his breath on her cheek, caught a whiff of onions. Clara stared at the splintered red wood. There was no door. It had gone, just like Robert. She fell to the side, her breaths coming too sharp and too fast. It felt as if someone had ironed her lungs flat and no amount of air she dragged through her lips would fully inflate them. Pain exploded through her chest and she closed her eyes.

Two men with bright torches were rooting through the rubble. "Is anyone alive?" they were yelling. "Shout if you're trapped."

The onion-breath man had his arms around her and was lifting her to her feet again. Clara was too weak to resist. "Fetch a stretcher. She's bleeding."

Poor girl, thought Clara numbly. *How awful to be hurt like that. What terrible luck*. Then with a jolt she realized he was talking about her.

"Look," shouted another voice.

Clara summoned all of her strength and lifted her head. The smoke and dust were clearing. A man was standing in the debris holding something aloft. The beam of a torch swept across it. The thing being held was spiky and familiar and made Clara's head and chest ache.

"A pineapple!" shouted the man in amazement.

"No," panted Clara.

"Won't be long now, love. Get you to hospital nice and quick," said the onion-breath man, cradling her in his arms. He smoothed her hair away from her cheeks, which were slick with sweat and tears.

"The pineapple," Clara said breathlessly, reaching out for it. She blinked the dust from her eyes and looked again for the man holding the fruit, but he had gone.

CHAPTER 39

Luck

The hand on Clara's forehead was cool and pleasant. She felt rather hot and feverish and the sheets were scratchy against her skin.

"The shrapnel cut was deep," murmured a man's voice. "She lost a lot of blood and she'll have a tremendous scar, but she'll recover well. We thought for a time she may have punctured a lung, but it was bruising to the ribs. She had a lucky escape."

A strange noise, a whimper, filtered into Clara's ears.

Her eyes flickered open.

Mrs Gilbert was leaning over her, gently stroking her forehead. "Oh," she whispered. She gave Clara a shaky smile. "You poor, poor girl. You gave us such a fright."

Clara turned her head. Mr Gilbert was sitting on the other side of the bed, his hands clasped together, almost as if he was praying. His eyes were bloodshot, his bird's-nest hair even more dishevelled than usual.

"Clara," he said simply.

The Zeppelin.

The bomb.

Robert.

The pineapple.

It all came flooding back like a tidal wave, knocking the little breath she had from her lungs. Clara turned her head to one side. Beds lined the room; crisp white sheets and hushed voices and the smell of something soapy and clean. She was in hospital.

"Your mother is on her way," Mrs Gilbert said softly. "She got the first train this morning. She'll arrive this evening."

Clara's throat felt thick, like she had swallowed a pot of glue. This evening? How long had she been asleep?

"Robert," she wheezed, looking at Mr Gilbert. "Kitty?" She placed a hand on her ribs, which felt tender, like the horse had been lying on them.

Mr Gilbert's face tightened. "Kitty is fine. The bombs

gave her a fright and she ran off, taking the cart with her. One of the boys found her down by the meadows. She's back at the stables. As for Robert…we don't know where he is."

Clara tried to push herself upright. Mrs Gilbert supported her and patted the pillows into shape. She waited for a minute or two for Clara to catch her breath. "That's it, nice and steady. Take deep breaths if you can," she said, stroking Clara's hair from her face. Mrs Gilbert's overworked fingers were gentle, and the gesture made Clara's ribs ache even more.

She closed her eyes and felt herself slipping into a dream where careful hands were lifting her hair and fastening something cool around her neck. Except it wasn't a dream. Her eyes jerked open and her fingers reached up to her throat. Mrs Gilbert's gold chain sat there, the cross nestling in the hollow of her neck.

Mrs Gilbert grasped Clara's other hand between hers and rubbed warmth into her stiff fingers. "I want you to have this necklace. I hope it will…keep you safe." Her lips tilted into a tiny smile.

Clara gave her a weak smile in return, her fingers sliding over the gold worn smooth by her aunt's touch. This was one of her aunt's most precious possessions,

had been with her in good times and bad. A sense of calm washed over Clara, like the palest of blue spring skies. She had a feeling she and her aunt could perhaps become friends in time.

Mrs Gilbert cleared her throat and plumped up Clara's pillows again (even though they really didn't need any more plumping). Mr Gilbert's eyes twinkled, and he patted Clara on the arm.

There was so much to be thankful for. And yet... "Robert was there. Then he wasn't," Clara whispered. "The bomb..."

Mrs Gilbert passed Clara a glass of water. She took a sip, letting the coolness soothe her sandpapery throat.

Mr Gilbert pulled a piece of paper from his pocket. It was the paper Clara had taken from Robert's jacket. A one-way passage to Brazil for a Mr Robert Wiltshire. Paid in full. The Royal Mail steamer was due to leave from Southampton the following week.

"One of the nurses found this in your pocket when you were brought to the hospital. She knew Robert, because he had been bringing the vegetables here. She left a message at the Big House to say a young girl had been injured, thinking you might work there. We put two and two together and realized it must be you. It was lucky. We would not have known what had happened to you otherwise."

Luck. Was this luck? Clara tried to piece it together in her head. All the decisions she had made had led her to this point. If she hadn't taken the papers from Robert's pocket, if she hadn't decided to follow him, would things have been different?

She took another sip of water and passed the glass to Mrs Gilbert. "There was a pineapple in the rubble."

Mrs Gilbert's lips thinned. "That blessed fruit. It has a lot to answer for," she said.

"Robert stole the fruit," Mr Gilbert said. "We know that now. The man who lived in the house which was bombed had been selling it on the black market. He's confessed to everything. He wasn't in at the time of the bombing – hadn't expected Robert until the following day. Robert used the money to pay for his passage abroad." Mr Gilbert paused. "Will wasn't the thief. But you did a foolish thing, Clara, following Robert like that. Things could have turned out…a lot worse."

The knot of anxiety in Clara's stomach loosened. "So Will is free?"

Mrs Gilbert nodded.

Clara slumped back on her pillows, grimacing at the

285

wave of pain which racked her body. The truth had been uncovered. She and Will had been right about Robert. He had lied to everyone. But the relief and gratification at knowing they were right did not course through her in the way she'd thought it would. Poor Will. Robert was a thief and now he was missing. Will had no one else in the world and nowhere to go. What was going to happen to him now?

CHAPTER 40

Scarlet Brazilian

Clara's mother hugged Clara so tightly, it squashed the breath from her lungs. "Oh that hurts… enough," Clara said weakly.

Her mother pulled away. Her eyes were watery. "Whatever have you been up to?" she murmured, clasping Clara's hands in hers. "Stolen fruit. A boy. A Zeppelin bomb. Shrapnel in your calf. Really, Clara, when I said have an adventure while staying with your aunt and uncle, this wasn't exactly what I had in mind."

"Father and Christopher – are they recovering?" Clara asked.

Her mother squeezed Clara's fingers. "They will be just fine. They will arrive next week."

Clara's insides jiggled. "What? Here?"

Clara's mother smiled. "Your uncle has found us a house on the Estate. You will be in hospital for a while. It will mean we can visit every day until you are well enough to come home to Kent with us. It will also mean Father can spend some time with his sister. I think they will both like that."

Clara thought about Frank, the small boy who had never had the chance to grow up and meet his distant Kentish relatives. She thought of her father, who was struggling to get over his experiences of the War. Maybe talking together about the horribleness of the last few years would help her aunt and her father – for, as she had learned, it was far better to talk about things that were bothering you than keep them hidden deep inside where they could fester and grow like weeds.

"I took a letter that came from the War Office. It was addressed to you and Father," said Clara, pulling away from her mother's grasp.

Clara's mother raised her eyebrows and sighed. "Elizabeth said. You just wanted to protect your father – and me." She pressed her fingers to her eyes. "It seems this war has made all of us determined to protect each other, in one way or another."

Clara let the thought settle into a spot under her sore ribs. Her parents had been trying to protect her by sending her to stay with her aunt and uncle. Her brother was trying to protect their country. She had been trying to protect Will. Mrs Gilbert had been trying to protect the memories of her dead nephew Frank. But what about Robert? He had only been trying to protect himself – running away from his mistakes, his responsibilities, from Will, from the death of their father.

Clara's mother glanced at the door.

Clara followed her gaze. "Will," she breathed.

Clara's mother smiled and beckoned him forward. He was clutching his cap in his hands. His eyes were heavy and dull, as if he had not slept.

"I will just…put these flowers in some water," Clara's mother said, picking up the sunshine-yellow dahlias she had brought and walking off to the nurses' station. She glanced over her shoulder and gave Clara an encouraging smile.

There was so much to be said, but where to start?

Will stood at the edge of the bed. He kept glancing at Clara's right leg, thick with creamy bandages.

"Does it hurt much?" he asked.

"A little," Clara said, deciding that he didn't need to know the whole truth.

"I'm sorry," Will said in a low voice.

"What? You have nothing to be sorry for," Clara replied croakily.

Will shuffled from foot to foot.

"Please sit, Will. You're making me nervous."

Will perched on the wooden chair, placed his cap down and rubbed his hands on his knees.

"I'm the one who should be sorry," Clara said. "If I hadn't followed Robert…maybe…"

"No," Will said firmly. "None of this is your doing. Robert made his own choices."

"I just wish they'd been the right ones," said Clara miserably.

Will nodded, looking at the floor. "There was only one steamer ticket. Robert wasn't planning on taking me with him. I searched his room. I thought there must be another hidden somewhere."

A nurse arrived at the bed next to Clara's and began to prepare the sheets, her confident hands smoothing and tucking them into place.

"You did a brave thing," Will said, his eyes meeting Clara's for the first time. They seemed to be full of pain and hurt, but also a little of something else – relief. "I would still be locked up if you hadn't pursued Robert."

Clara tucked her hair behind her ears. "I'm not the brave one, Will. You are."

A flush stole up Will's neck. He tugged at his collar.

"There's been no word from Robert, then? Mr Gilbert said…he was not found in the bomb blast," said Clara.

Will shook his head. "He didn't return to the estate. He's vanished."

"Why?" Clara asked.

Will shrugged and leaned forward in his chair. "Same reason he stole the fruits, I think. He couldn't cope when Father died. The responsibility…looking after me. He's angry he can't enlist because of his eye, not able to accept that was of his own doing. He wants to escape. Maybe he just needs a little time on his own. Maybe he will come back for me then?" Will glanced at Clara. Hope was burning brightly in his eyes.

Could he be right? Would Robert return? If he did, he would face questioning by the police, probably time in prison. But surely the strength of love he had for Will would outweigh all of that? Clara hoped so. But then she remembered the first time she had met Robert in the hothouses, how he had spoken dreamily of faraway places, tropical beaches. How he had lied to her about his injured eye. How he had given Will the responsibility of burying their father's things and left him to take the blame for the thieving. How he hadn't paid Red the hall boy for covering for them. Robert wasn't who Will thought he was. But that was for Will to come to terms with in his own time. And when he did, Clara was going to be right there to help him.

"What will you do now?" Clara asked, gingerly pressing on her bandage.

"The Gilberts have taken me in."

Clara looked at Will in surprise. "What? You're staying at the cottage?"

Will nodded. "In your attic room. You…don't mind, do you?"

Clara shook her head, then told him about her parents coming to stay on the Estate until she was well enough to go home. "I liked being in the attic. It made me feel…small…but at the same time part of something bigger, what with the way the room overlooked the gardens and the hothouses and all the busyness."

"Yes, you do get a good view of the hothouses," said Will with a smile. "You never know what, or rather who, you might see from up there."

"Quite," said Clara, raising her eyebrows and remembering the first time she had seen Will emerge from the hothouses in a halo of steam. Even though she was pleased for him, the thought of Will living in her attic room made her feel slightly odd, like it was the end of something she was not quite ready for. She sank back onto her pillows and stared up at the bare (and very high) hospital ceiling. "I hope Mrs Gilbert doesn't dust away the spiders between the attic beams," Clara said. "I liked watching them build their webs."

"They're still there," said Will. "They've as much right to be there as me or you, and it's nice to have their company."

Clara smiled. The attic room had been a safe place for her to stay, but it was Will's turn to feel safe now.

"Mr Gilbert has given me some work on the Estate," Will said, his voice a little brighter.

"In the hothouses?"

"No," Will said wistfully. "But maybe one day, if I work hard enough. He wanted to see my notebooks. Said I had some good ideas."

"That's wonderful," said Clara, her smile broadening to ache her cheeks.

Clara's mother returned then with the vase of

flowers. "I think that's enough talking for one day." She placed the vase on the table next to Clara's bed. "Oh, I almost forgot." She took a hastily wrapped brown-paper parcel from her bag and placed it on Clara's lap. "It's from the Earl."

Clara wrinkled her nose. "The Earl? Have you met him?"

"Yes, he was in the gardens visiting the hothouses and…the tree stump." Clara's mother gave her a careful glance, implying that Mrs Gilbert had told her of the tragedy of young Frank. "The Earl is arranging for some men to dig out the stump. He's asked the gardeners to grow soft fruits there – strawberries and raspberries. He really is a very nice man."

Yes, thought Clara. *He really is*. Mrs Gilbert would like that; a sweet-smelling and useful place she could go and remember Frank, rather than the horrid tree stump to remind her of that tragic day.

Clara rested the Earl's parcel on the bed and carefully pulled back the paper. There sat a single fat pineapple. Will drew in a breath. "A Scarlet Brazilian."

Clara picked it up and turned it over in her hands, the quilted prickles digging into her skin. It was heavy and ripe.

Will grinned.

"The Earl did say something rather odd," Clara's mother said. "He said to tell you he hopes you make a quick recovery…and that he had just finished the latest Sherlock Holmes novel, and that it was jolly good. Something about…lost evidence?"

A small smile stole onto Clara's lips.

Will looked at her quizzically. "What is it?"

"Oh, nothing," she said.

Other patients and their visitors were looking over and whispering. "A pineapple," one lady said to the man she was visiting. "Looks home-grown too."

"Shall I see if the nurse has a knife and a plate?" Clara's mother asked lightly, her head tilted.

Will leaned forward on his chair. This wasn't the picture Clara had in her head, of her and Will on a sunny day, silver trays and fine china, the breeze whipping their hair as they bit into the sweet yellow flesh. But as she had learned, life had a habit of changing your plans without giving you any notice at all.

"That would be perfect," Clara said to her mother, passing the pineapple to Will. Something swelled inside her chest. "Please can you ask for a few plates though," she said, glancing up and down the ward. "I think there will be enough for everyone, don't you?"

My inspiration behind writing
The Garden of Lost Secrets

When I was young, if anyone asked me whether I liked history, I laughed and said, "Absolutely not". To me, history meant old people sitting in darkened rooms with piles of boring, musty-smelling books. Thinking about the people who lived in my house before me, wishing I could peel back the past like the skin of an orange so I could talk to them – that was certainly not history. Reading books like *Little Women* by Louisa May Alcott, and desperately wishing for a time machine to take me back to nineteenth-century America, did not mean I liked history.

Except, you've probably guessed by now, that in fact all of those things did mean I enjoyed history – I was just experiencing it in a different way to sitting in a musty book-filled room! What this taught me is that there is no right or wrong way to enjoy learning about the past – all you really need is an imagination to take you there. If you could imagine yourself back in time to visit one place, where would that be? Would it be your house, a local park, or your school? Could you perhaps find an old map of this place online and compare it to a map of the area today? You might be amazed at what you find!

When I decided to write a story set during The Great War at Ickworth Estate in Suffolk, I wanted to do some historical research so my plot and the characters were realistic. I'm still not too keen on spending hours trawling through books, but instead find that visiting places often gives me brilliant writing inspiration. I took a tour of the servants' quarters at Ickworth house, keeping the dark, almost underground feel of the winding corridors in my mind as I wrote about Clara's desperate search to find Will after he had been taken to the cellars.

The pineapple houses in the walled gardens at Ickworth are currently sealed off to visitors for safety reasons, so I visited Cambridge's Botanical Gardens where there are some lovely hothouses which are still in use (although sadly they don't grow pineapples there). I spent time listening to the drips of condensation, breathing in the muggy, earthy air and imagining how Clara and Will would feel sitting in there alone in the dark. But one of the best bits of my research must be all of the pineapples I have bought and tasted – squat ones, thin ones, sweet ones and sour ones! The historical research I've done for this book has been interesting, rewarding, and tasty, and I very much hope that you enjoyed meeting Clara and Will and reading about their adventures in *The Garden of Lost Secrets*.

Ann-Marie Howell

Look out for A. M. Howell's next
thrilling historical mystery...

The House of
One Hundred Clocks

1905, a time of invention and change. Twelve-year-old Helena's
father is appointed clock-winder to Mr Harris – one of the
wealthiest men in the East of England – and his enormous
collection of clocks.

It's a risky job – if the clocks stop, Helena's father will lose
everything. But when Helena starts helping out, she discovers
the house of one hundred clocks is hiding many secrets, and
soon finds herself in a race against time to discover the truth…

Coming 2020

Book Club Questions

- Why do you think Clara decides not to open the letter from the War Office, even though she knows it might have important information in it? Is she scared? Devious? Secretive?

- During the First World War, lots of men were sent to fight in the army, which meant that women and girls had to fill some of their roles at home and in the workplace. Looking at pages 42, 59 and 164, talk about some of the jobs women were expected to step into. Was it a surprise to you that they weren't allowed or able to do these before? Why? Can you think of any other jobs or roles that women took on at this time?

- Clara's father tells her: "You are brave. And when you are brave, you can be anything you want to be... A dog-sledding explorer travelling over snow-capped mountains, a hot-air balloonist soaring over scorched deserts, a botanist making fantastical discoveries in the Amazonian jungle." Close your eyes and imagine what you could be, then talk to a friend and ask them what they imagined.

- *The Garden of Lost Secrets* was inspired by the discovery of a 100-year-old gardener's notebook. After reading Ann-Marie's letter on what inspired her to write this story, discuss whether you have ever visited somewhere that inspired you to think about the past, or found something that sparked the beginning of an idea for a story?

- In the early twentieth century, pineapples were very sought-after, as they weren't often grown in England and so had to be imported from abroad. As she looks at the fruit in the Earl's hothouses, Clara is desperate to taste one of the pineapples grown there. Think about what a pineapple looks like – do you think you could imagine what it might taste like from the smell and how it looks?

- In the book, we find fruit going missing as well as fruit appearing, with the mandarins that Clara finds on the tree stump. Who did you think was stealing the fruit, and who did you think was leaving the mandarins? Were you surprised when you found out who was really behind this?

- We discover at the end that Robert has been plotting to run away for a while. Did this come as a shock to you? Can you find any passages or hints that might suggest Robert isn't as trustworthy as he seems?

- Why do you think the author, A. M. Howell, has chosen to write the story from the third-person perspective? Would the story feel different if it had been from a first-person perspective? Could you imagine it told from Will's perspective, or even the Earl's or Robert's or Mrs Gilbert's perspectives?

Acknowledgements

I'm a firm believer that things happen for a reason and the reason I am writing these acknowledgments at all is down to my amazing agent Clare Wallace and the lovely Lydia Silver at Darley Anderson. Thanks for the pep talks, the constant belief and unwavering support – this would not be half as much fun without you by my side!

A huge thank you to the dream team at Usborne who helped get this book ready to go out into the world, but in particular to my editors Rebecca and Becky who are simply the best. I was overwhelmed from the start with the love you had for Clara and Will and their adventures – it's the stuff dreams are made of! Thanks also to Sarah Stewart – your copyedits were a revelation and joy to work on. I'm already counting down the days until we do it again. The gardens have been brought to life more perfectly than I could ever have imagined through the fabulous artwork – an enormous thank you to Katharine Millichope for the beautiful cover design and Amy Grimes for her lovely illustrations. The Usborne publicity and marketing team also need a special mention – in particular Katarina Jovanovic, Mariesa Dulak and PR consultant Fritha Lindqvist. Your publicity and marketing ideas are genius and I am forever grateful for all the time and care you put into promoting this book.

Thank you to Curtis Brown Creative and Catherine Johnson (author extraordinaire) and my fellow coursemates on the 2015 Writing YA and Children's Fiction course, for the feedback, laughs and encouragement. This course opened my eyes to the world of writing, publishing and agents and was the push I needed to begin believing.

To the lovely Doomsday Writers – thanks for the chats and for keeping me sane through the ups and downs of the last few years. I truly believe every writer should have a group like this on prescription.

Thanks to Sam, Darren and Serena, my fellow Usborne 2019 debut authors. It's been a real treat getting to know you guys. Our chats about all things writing and publishing have helped no end!

Without Ickworth Estate and gardens, there would be no story, so a huge thanks to the staff at the National Trust, in particular Sean Reid who so generously gave me a tour of the walled gardens and talked about the discovery of the notebook. Thanks also to the staff at Ickworth House for letting me "borrow" their excellent words for Mrs Gilbert's blackboard and for the inspiring visitor tour of the servants' quarters that gave me a glimpse into Clara's world.

To my dear Mum and Dad. Thank you for all the books and endless trips to the library when I was young. You enthusiastically fed my love of stories and writing, and I'll be forever grateful.

A heartfelt thanks to my boys Jack and Ed. Thanks for putting up with my grumpiness when the writing wasn't going so well and the late dinners when it was going too well. I promise not to talk about plots, characters, or my next book over mealtimes (so much).

A final thank you must go to my lovely husband Jeremy. Your generous and whole-hearted encouragement means the world to me. I remember you once saying I had a book in me, and you were right!

USBORNE QUICKLINKS

For links to websites where you can find out more about the First World War and other historical events in this book, go to the Usborne Quicklinks website at www. usborne.com/quicklinks and type in the title of this book.

At Usborne Quicklinks you can:

- Find out what life was like for soldiers during the First World War
- Watch video clips about life on the home front
- Learn more about the role of women, and women's rights at the time of the First World War
- See photos of Ickworth House, a country estate in England, and the inspiration for the setting of the story

Please follow the online safety guidelines at the Usborne Quicklinks website.